CAN THIS BE ME

Time After Time

MARGARET TEEGARDEN

Can This Be Me: Time After Time

ISBN

979-8-89175-213-9 (sc)

979-8-89175-217-7 (hc)

979-8-89175-214-6 (e)

To my readers.

I want to Thank You for reading my book.
I hope you enjoy the story as much as I did writing it.

I also want to dedicate my writings to my Family.

My husband, Bob. My three Children, Fred, Lucy and Nikki.
Grandchildren, Kandi, Wayne, Amanda, Robbie, Tiffanie and Faith.
Also my Great Grandchildren, Allixandria, Amiyah,
Adrian, Chloe, Bella, Harlee, and Navey.

God Bless them all.

CONTENTS

PROLOGUE

Imagine being a child of four years old and finding yourself in a shallow creek. How did you get there? You don't really know or understand. You know only that you were pushed. But by who—or what? There was no one there, nothing to see. Yet here you are, in the water, struggling to reach the surface. You can't breathe. Your head is being forced under by some unseen force. Your lungs fill with water, and you feel the battle slipping away. Even at four years old, you know enough to realize: you are dying. Life is slowly fading. Then comes the dark before the light. Somehow, you find yourself sitting on the creek bank, shivering, cold, and covered with mud. It all seems like a bad dream—but you know it isn't. At the very last instant of your tiny life, something saved you. *Why?*

This is the life of Christy. She lived a happy childhood, never truly understanding what happened that day. But as she grows older, trouble follows. She is tormented by voices that only she can hear. The voices call to her, commanding her to follow. As a child, she can control them. But as she matures, the voices grow stronger, more insistent. As they dominate her life, she begins to slip away. When she relaxes, she travels—mentally—to another time and another life, a past life. In these lives, she always dies a tragic death. She becomes the person of that life, feeling their pain and agony in their final moments. And when they die, Christy snaps back to her own reality.

Christy is now a mother and a wife. She struggles to live a normal life despite her problems. But the more she resists the voices, the more powerful they become. Her family seeks professional help, only to be told that there is no solution. They insist she must be institutionalized. The voices grow angry. They have a mission that Christy must fulfill: *she must die.* Armed with knowledge of the future, the voices lead Christy to places where death seems inevitable. Yet she is always saved, only to confront the face of death again and again.

Finally, the voices gain complete control. All hope seems lost. Christy appears doomed to a certain death. Or is there a force more powerful than the one tormenting her? In the final pages, you will find the answers. And you, the reader, will be the judge: do miracles exist?

CHAPTER
One

Family Tragedy

It's a cool, crisp early spring morning in March. All the farmhands are out in the fields preparing them for the spring plowing.

You can smell the fresh fertilizer as they spread it across the fields and gardens. The men working the fields are called sharecroppers. They help plant and harvest the crops. At harvest time, they share the crops and any profits that may be made.

The men don't always get along, sometimes causing fights. Some are lazy and try to push the workload onto others, while others work their fingers to the bone to get the job done. The ones who work the hardest usually have families to feed.

Jake is one of the hardest workers. He has a wife and two children to feed, with another due any day. Jake's mother lives with Jake and his wife, Ellan, since Jake's father was killed in an occupational accident.

Jake's father worked for a mining company stripping coal. Jobs were scarce and times were really hard after World War II. Everyone had to live on rations. They used ration stamps for gasoline, sugar, flour, and many other items necessary for survival. People did what they had to do to get by during those difficult times.

It's been almost four years since Jake's father died. Jake remembers the day very well.

Jake and his brother Tom stayed up all night helping their father fix tires on their old car so their father, John, could get to work the next day. John left for work the next morning at about five o'clock. He had to be on the job at seven, and the car didn't run very well, so he had to leave early.

All three of them were tired that morning. They hadn't gotten any sleep, but they did what they had to do.

Jake and Tom watched their father drive up the lane and out of sight. The old car spit, coughed, and backfired as he went around the turn at the top of the hill.

The boys were tired and hungry, so they went back to the house.

The boys went to the kitchen to see what their mother was fixing for breakfast. Mary had homemade pancakes and syrup on the stove. She also had fresh sausage from the pig they had butchered the day before.

Breakfast was great. Mary was an excellent cook.

After breakfast, they had a lot of chores to do. It was late October and the days were getting shorter, so the work had to be done while the sun was still up. Besides that, Jake had plans for the evening.

He had asked the girl who lived on the next farm to go to the local dance with him. Her name was Ellan. She was a real beauty—long dark hair, big blue eyes, and a beautiful figure. Jake had fallen in love as soon as he saw her.

He found himself wishing he could do more than just take her to the dance, but he couldn't because he didn't have the money. He only had enough to get them there.

Jake decided not to worry about that now. They had a lot of work to do, so they'd better get started or they wouldn't get it finished.

Jake and Tom went out the door toward the barn.

They started with the milking. That took the longest. By the time they rounded up the cows and finished milking, it was around noon.

After the milking was done, they worked in the stalls. They all needed cleaning, and that was quite a job. They were about halfway through when Jake took a little breather. He went to the barn door and leaned on his pitchfork, staring out over the back meadow.

The scenery was beautiful this time of year. Late October in southwestern Pennsylvania is a good time to appreciate Mother Nature's gifts. The trees were a magical sight—brilliant reds and oranges. Funny, Jake had never paid much attention to them before. He must be in love.

Jake was in another world. He didn't know what was going on around him. He had Ellan on his mind and the dance that evening. Jake simply forgot how tired he was and just stood there gazing out the door.

But he was soon brought back to reality—real quick. In his absent-minded state, he had forgotten to close the stall door he had just cleaned. One of the team workhorses had gotten out and nearly ran Jake down. The horse, feeling pretty frisky, wanted to run—and run he did.

He raced across the pasture and jumped the fence leading to the meadow, with Jake in hot pursuit. The young colt was enjoying his freedom. Whenever Jake got too close, the horse ran harder. The horse wanted to play, and the more Jake chased him, the faster he ran.

Jake was very tired and frustrated, but finally, after a long chase, the horse had enough and came to Jake on his own. Jake led him back to the stall and gave him his hay.

"Now it's lunchtime," Jake called to Tom, and they headed to the house.

Back in the house, Mary was baking homemade bread and pies—apple and cherry, Jake's favorites.

While Mary worked, her mind began to wander, and she felt a little depressed. They had saved thousands of dollars in a local bank but lost all of it when the bank folded after the war. Before the bank closed, they had been feeling pretty secure. They had money in the bank and hope for the future.

After that, they lost the farm and nearly everything they owned. Now they lived in this run-down place, and if they didn't work hard to keep things up, it might just fall down around their ears.

But Mary was content. She knew that John would take care of the things that needed repairing. He would never let her down without good reason. John was a good man, and Mary just wished she could do more to help, but she already had her hands full with the farm and five children.

Mary smiled as she thought of her husband and felt a great sense of pride in him. She loved him very much.

"Time to get back to work," she thought. The day was getting shorter, and there were still many things to be done.

The day wore on, and it was finally supper time. Jake was really getting excited now about the dance. In a little while, he would be getting ready to pick up Ellan.

Tom and his sisters teased Jake about his date. Jake got angry, and Mary had to settle the argument.

"It's supper time," she said. "Your father will be home soon. Girls, set the table. Jake and Tom, bring in some firewood."

They did as they were told. Mary was still a little angry about the argument, but it was settled now.

It was about six o'clock, and John was about a half hour late. Mary didn't worry much. She knew the old car was contrary and sometimes gave him trouble on the road.

The car didn't always start without a jump. Time passed, and it was really dark now—about seven o'clock.

Jake was getting nervous. He needed the car for his date, so he and Tom went out on the porch to wait for their father.

About fifteen minutes went by when they saw car lights coming down the lane. As the car got closer, the boys realized it wasn't their father. It was the sheriff from Hickory.

Tom and Jake felt weak and a little sick to their stomachs. They knew something was wrong.

They stood and watched as two men got out of the car. The men walked up to the porch and asked the boys if they could speak with Mary. Jake invited them in while Tom went to get his mother.

The two men waited quietly in the doorway. Tom came back and said his mother would be right with them.

A few minutes later, Mary came down the hall. She looked pale. She already knew something was terribly wrong.

The sheriff spoke gently.

"Hello, ma'am. I'm sorry to bring bad news, but there was an accident this afternoon, and your husband was killed."

Mary gasped and fell to the floor. The men helped the boys get Mary to the couch while the girls brought towels to wipe her face. She finally came out of her state of shock and started to cry. Her heart was breaking.

"You must be mistaken," she said. "My husband will be home soon. It's that damn car. It doesn't run right, you know."

The sheriff came over and sat beside Mary.

"No, ma'am, we're not mistaken," he said gently. "Your husband is dead. I'm terribly sorry."

John was about to wrap things up for the day when the shift changed. He was walking to his car when he noticed the steam shovel start up. He didn't pay much attention to it because he had been working around it all day.

John stopped to talk to the shovel operator whose shift had just ended. The man told John he was glad to be going home — and that John should be, too.

John asked why.

The man said the other shovel operator was an ass and that he was in a drunken stupor. Someone was going to get hurt.

The man said good night to John. "I'm out of here. See you tomorrow."

John said good night and headed toward his car. He was almost there when he realized he had forgotten his shovel and pick, so he went back to get them. He needed them to do his job. They were stripping coal, and the work would be impossible without his tools. He couldn't afford to lose them.

John had just picked up his tools when he noticed the steam shovel running faster. The shovel operator had passed out over the controls. He had fallen onto the throttle.

The shovel began turning at a terrible rate of speed. When it suddenly stopped, it jerked violently. The machine had turned faster than it was capable of, and when it came to an abrupt stop, the cable snapped.

The shovel flew through the air.

It was heading straight toward John.

John tried to run from it, but the speed of the shovel was too great. He couldn't outrun it. The shovel landed squarely on top of him, pinning him to the ground.

The men ran to him, trying to help. John looked at them, pain written across his face.

One of the men, a close friend of John's, screamed, "Get an ambulance! This man needs help!"

John looked up at his friend, and the man watched the life slowly leave him.

When help finally arrived, John was already dead. They told his friend there was nothing anyone could have done for him. He had been crushed from the chest down.

The men then went to the shovel to get the man who had been operating it. They were furious and wanted to kill him.

The sheriff arrived before they had a chance to seriously hurt him. The operator was arrested and taken to jail for involuntary manslaughter and reckless endangerment.

But they really didn't have to punish the man. He had to live with what he had done. He had another man's blood on his hands, and he couldn't deal with the guilt. In time, he lost his mind.

But even then, there was no way to right the wrong that had been done to Mary and her family.

CHAPTER
Two

The Voices Are Calling

Mary now faced the most difficult time in her life. She had always believed John would be there forever. *My God,* she thought. *What do I do? I have no idea where to start.*

Mary went to her mother and father's home. They were elderly, but they stood by their daughter all the way in her time of need.

Mary had no money to spare. What little she had was needed to feed her family. The coal company helped by paying for the funeral and the gravesite. Mary chose the cemetery where both of their grandparents were buried.

Now she had to prepare for the ordeal of getting five children ready to say their final farewell to their father.

Jake and Tom were the oldest of the children. The younger ones were girls. The boys had a terrible time trying to help get things ready for the funeral. The children had to deal with their loss while also helping Mary cope with hers. It wasn't easy during such a tragic time.

Jake, in total despair over everything that had happened, never got to see Ellan that night. He hoped she didn't think he had simply stood her up.

But he didn't need to worry.

When Ellan heard the news, she was there through it all. She helped with the younger children and stayed right by the family's side. Ellan and Jake's families became very close.

Jake was definitely in love.

After the funeral, Mary had to try to keep things together. After two or three months, she had to let the farm go—she just couldn't make it without John. Although she received a small pension from the coal company, it was not enough to make ends meet.

Mary thought about John every day, and her heart ached. She missed him terribly. But she had to move on with her life— for the children's sake.

Mary went to see her parents; she needed their help. They told her not to worry: she and the children could come live with them. They said that if she did, she would also be helping them. They needed some young people around to help out anyway. The boys could help on the farm, and Mary and the girls could help her mother with chores around the house.

Things worked out well for about a year, until Mary noticed that her mother was failing. She became very ill. The doctor said it was just a matter of time. Almost two weeks later, her mother passed away.

Now the family had to deal with another loss. With all the grief of losing his wife, Mary's father was failing, too. Mary really had her hands full. She basically had to run the farm herself. It was more than she could reasonably handle, but she hung in there and did the best she could.

Even with the help of all the children, things did not get any better.

One morning, Jake came to talk to his mother. He wanted to ask if she would consent to him and Ellan getting married.

Mary said, "That's absurd! You're both just children. You're too young, and I will not allow it."

But being too young had nothing to do with Mary's answer. The real reason was that she was being selfish—thinking only of herself and not the happiness of the two young lovers. She didn't want to lose a son, even though she loved Ellan very much.

Mary's answer made Jake furious. He told her, "Like it or not, I am going to marry Ellan anyway."

Jake did not tell Mary that he had to marry Ellan because she was three months pregnant. But that didn't matter—they wanted to get married regardless. So they eloped to the state of Virginia and were married the following week.

Mary wasn't happy about the whole idea, but she got used to it. She even started thinking about being a grandmother and kind of liked the idea after all.

Jake found a job right after he and Ellan returned from Virginia. About ten miles outside of Hickory was a huge farm. The owner of the farm hired men to work under a share system. Jake and Ellan lived in a small tenant house on the farm and paid very little rent. It was the most logical arrangement, allowing Jake not to travel back and forth to work.

Some time passed, and Mary's father passed away. All the other children had moved out on their own. Mary was left alone, so she came to live with Ellan and Jake. Mary helped out with her small pension, and Jake worked the farm.

This arrangement helped everyone. It allowed Jake and Ellan to meet their bills, and Ellan had the extra hand she needed with the children.

Jake had almost completed a day's work—just two more rows to plow, and he could call it a day. The horses were tired and restless. They had worked hard under the heat, plowing field after field, row after row, and they deserved an extra helping of hay that night.

Completely worn out, Jake stopped to take a breather. He stood for a few minutes, watching toward the house. He saw someone running across the field but couldn't quite make out who it was—until he heard his mother's voice. He knew instantly that something was wrong.

He handed the team of horses to his helper and ran toward his mother. When he reached Mary, she was ready to collapse. She was winded but managed to tell Jake that the baby was coming.

Jake made sure Mary was okay and then headed to the house. Mary followed shortly after and went to check on Ellan to see how much time they had. She told Jake to get the other two children out to play and to go fetch the doctor.

Nervous but determined, Jake did exactly as his mother instructed. He went for the doctor and returned alone. Mary was relieved to see him.

"You had better boil some water," she said. "The baby seems to think we don't need the doctor. It's ready now, and we have to help Ellan."

Jake hesitated, but Mary urged him on. "Come on, Jake. Ellan needs us—and she needs us now." She told him to gather water and as many towels as he could find.

They thought everything would be over soon. But Ellan was in labor for a long time. She screamed in pain, and Jake was getting really scared. *God, where's the doctor?* he thought. He went outside to bring the children in, feed them their supper, and get them ready for bed.

Once the children were tucked in, Mary came to ask him where the doctor was. Jake explained that the doctor's wife had told him the doctor was on an emergency call and that she would send him as soon as he returned.

Mary ran back to the bedroom with Ellan, while Jake tried to settle the children. It was almost impossible with Ellan screaming and making so much noise in the other room. Finally, Jake got the children in bed and went into the kitchen to sit down for a few minutes.

Soon, he heard Mary shouting, "Push, Ellan, push! We're almost there—hang in there and push!"

It wasn't long before Jake heard a baby crying. He ran to the bedroom door and went in. Mary looked up, wiped the blood from her hands, and said, "It's a girl—a beautiful little girl with blonde hair and blue eyes."

It was 10:45, and the doctor had just arrived. Jake told him the baby had already been born. The doctor went straight into the bedroom to see Ellan and the baby. He congratulated Mary on the fine job she had done and teased her about trying to take over his work.

"Fat chance of that," Mary said with a smile. She really didn't like the job, but she was proud of her effort. She left the room, smiling.

Jake looked at the children, now asleep, and thought about how lucky he was. He had two little girls and one boy, all healthy, and all part of his growing family.

Jake left the children's bedroom and went to see Ellan and the new baby. Ellan smiled at him when he entered the room. She looked tired and sweaty, but to Jake, she was still beautiful.

The doctor said, "Not too long, Jake—they need to rest."

Jake kissed Ellan and asked how she felt. She said she was okay and handed the little bundle to him. He looked at the baby and visibly swelled with pride.

Ellan said she would like to name the baby after his mother, if that was okay with him. Jake smiled—he was very happy. The baby was named Mary Christine, and they called her Christy for short.

Jake kissed Ellan and the baby goodnight and left the room. He joined Mary and the doctor in the kitchen. The doctor reassured him, saying that both Ellan and the baby were fine. What none of them knew was that Christy was different in a small, subtle way.

Days turned into weeks, and weeks into years. The children grew, and now there were five of them. Christy was four years old.

It was mid-summer in 1952, and Jake and Ellan were getting ready for a family reunion. They packed their blankets and picnic basket into the car for the long drive.

The reunion was held at a beautiful location. A covered bridge spanned a shallow but wide creek. The children could play by the creek without the parents worrying too much about them drowning. The banks were lined with wildflowers, and the fragrance of the blossoms was refreshing. Everything was green and vibrant. It was a glorious day for a picnic.

The festivities began around noon. There were games to play—sack races, baseball, hog chasing, and many more. Later, a country band played, so that after all the games, everyone could gather by the fire or dance in the moonlight.

It was evening, and everyone was having a good time. Mary came to Jake and Ellan and asked if they had seen Christy. They realized they hadn't seen her for some time, so they all started looking for her. One of the little boys said he had seen her heading toward the creek.

Jake became upset; he just wanted to find Christy. He ran down toward the creek, up one side and down the other. Then he went to look under the bridge. That's where he found her— soaking wet and covered in mud.

Jake was relieved. He picked her up, hugged her, and kissed her. "What were you doing under the bridge by yourself? Were you lost, honey?" he asked.

"No, Daddy," Christy said. "They were calling me, and I couldn't find them. They called me into the water and told me they would be there, but I couldn't find them."

Christy was sobbing and trembling.

"Who, honey? Who called you into the water?" Jake asked.

"The voices, Daddy," she whispered. "They always talk to me. They call my name all the time."

Jake thought it was just an overactive imagination and took Christy back to the others. Ellan dried her off and put clean clothes on her. They returned to the dance, and this time Christy stayed with them while Mary watched her as Jake and Ellan danced.

Later in the evening, Christy was sitting on Mary's lap and almost fell asleep when she suddenly jumped up. Mary heard her say, "I'm coming."

"Christy, honey, who are you talking to?" Mary asked.

"Them, Gramma. They're calling me again," Christy replied.

Mary said, "Ignore them, honey, and they'll go away." From that moment, Christy learned at a young age to ignore the voices—and if Gramma said it was okay, then it was okay. From that time on, no one knew that the voices were an ongoing problem for Christy. She did an excellent job of covering them up, almost as if they didn't exist.

CHAPTER
Three

The Problems Start Again

Some time had passed. Jake and Ellan now had eight children—four boys and four girls. Christy was a teenager, still living her secret life, but outwardly, she was a normal teenager in every way. She excelled in her studies and was very popular with other students. She had many friends and plenty of dates if she chose, but most of the boys she wouldn't give the time of day, let alone a date. Most of them just wanted a hot date—and Christy was no one's "hot date." She preferred to spend a lot of time alone. **This was when she became very different.**

On one particular occasion, Christy sat in a quiet place to relax. She breathed deeply several times, closed her eyes, and let her mind drift. Pictures appeared in her mind's eye—images of a place she did not know.

The air was muggy and hot; she could feel the moisture clinging to her skin. Something soft—grass or dirt—was beneath her bare feet. She smelled smoke and looked around, realizing there was a fire burning in the middle of a small village. Christy did not recognize the place, but she instinctively knew it was a native village. Small bamboo huts surrounded her.

She could hear the pounding of drums. Panic erupted all around her, and from the way the villagers were running, she sensed danger. She did not know what kind, but there was screaming, and women were fleeing into the forest with their children. She was right—the village was under attack.

Christy felt terror as she watched the attackers kill the men and drag off the women and children. Something tugged at her leg. She realized these must be her children.

She grabbed the two little ones and tried to run. Her legs pumped as fast as they could, but it felt hopeless. She ran deep into the jungle, but the enemy was closing in. Her heart pounded, her chest ached, and every muscle ached. She could not stop, for if she did, she would surely die. She would not let them take her alive.

She ran harder, up to a cliff. *Oh God, nowhere to go,* she thought. She decided to try climbing down. She started over the edge, but the weight of the children made it almost impossible. Yet she would never let them fall into the hands of the enemy. She resolved that if they were to die, they would die together.

She climbed a little further down the cliff. The attackers were getting closer, faster now. She tried to hold on, but her grip began to slip—and then she felt the searing pain as she was falling.

She remembers every time she hit a rock or ledge on the way down. The children broke loose from her arms, and she could see their little bodies bouncing off the rocks below. She hit some trees near the bottom and felt like she was cut in half.

The final hit was on her shoulder, then her head. Those few seconds seemed like hours.

As she lay at the bottom of the cliff, she opened her eyes. *The pain was terrible.* She looked at the sky, which was turning very dark—darker and darker—until it finally faded away. *The native girl dies.*

When it was over, Christy snapped back to reality. She was shaking and covered with sweat. She was terrified. Christy thought she would get used to this after a while, since it happened all the time. But with each occurrence, the visions became more graphic and real. Christy felt more fear and pain with each one. She was confused and scared, and as she wiped the sweat from her face, she thought, *"MY GOD... WAS THAT ME?"*

Christy learned to cope with her problem. She tried her gramma's theory: ignore it, and it will go away. It didn't work entirely, but it helped her manage. Life was not easy for Christy at this point. She had to drop out of school to help care for her brothers and sisters while Ellan went to work to support the family.

Mary no longer lived with Jake and Ellan. She had moved next door to one of her daughters. Ellan needed help, and Christy, being the eldest at home, naturally had to take responsibility. Christy didn't mind—she had lost interest in school anyway. She felt so different from everyone else. She was becoming a loner, withdrawn from all her friends. Her friends had no idea why; they thought Christy had become a snob who considered herself too good for them. *If they only knew* the torment Christy was going through, they might understand. She considered it a blessing in disguise. As long as she helped out and kept busy, she had no time to dwell on her fears or live her own quiet life.

Life was different now for Jake and Ellan. With so many children to feed and money scarce, even with both working, tensions ran high. Jake became short-tempered and harsh. He was no longer the proud, patient father he had once been. He often got angry at the children and punished them for trivial mistakes. He and Ellan fought constantly over money and bills.

They did receive some assistance with food through family surplus programs. When qualified, they would stand in the surplus lines on a first-come, first-served basis. They received cheese, flour, cornmeal, lard, canned pork and beef, and even dried beans. Gramma Mary could turn navy beans and dumplings with homemade bread into an exciting meal, and all the children loved when she visited.

Even though Mary no longer lived with Jake and Ellan, she still spent time with the family. She missed the children, and Christy got some relief from her chores while Mary was there. Mary would have continued living with Jake's family if it weren't for Jake's sisters. They resented him, claiming he was taking advantage of Mary's small income. They insisted that Mary live alone in a small two-room bungalow, and she did—but she wasn't happy. That's why she still spent so much time with Jake's family.

Christy's oldest brother brought a friend home one day. They were planning to work on her brother's car. Her brother introduced Christy to Sam. Sam was tall, dark, and handsome, and Christy felt an instant connection. She didn't meet many new people these days; she was too busy helping with the family. Her oldest sister was married now, and life was especially tough on Christy.

Jake and Ellan didn't get much time together these days, which was fine—at least they didn't have time to fight. So, needless to say, Sam was a welcome and refreshing presence for Christy. He started spending a lot of time with Christy's brother, Carl, but it was obvious to everyone that he was really interested in Christy.

Jake did not approve of Sam, so Christy and Sam had to be careful when they were together. Jake would have been furious if he knew how close they were. He believed Sam was a lowlife and not good enough for Christy. Of course, Christy didn't agree. Since Carl had a girlfriend, Sam could spend time with Christy whenever Carl was busy on the phone or otherwise occupied.

Sam was older than Christy by five years, and he seemed confident around girls. Christy, being shy and inexperienced, felt both nervous and excited around him. Her life had been so busy with family that she hadn't spent much time thinking about romance.

One day, Sam came over and wanted to spend some time alone with Christy. She sent the younger children outside to play, and they were finally alone. Sam took her hand gently and led her to the spare attic room, which was cozy and quiet.

Christy's palms were sweaty, and she felt shy, but she trusted him. Sam smiled and whispered, "I like you, Christy. I promise I'll always respect you." She blushed and felt a warmth in her chest she had never felt before. They talked for hours, sharing their hopes and dreams, laughing at small jokes, and holding hands.

By the end of the afternoon, Christy realized she had never felt so cared for. Sam's kindness and attention made her feel special and grown-up, and though she was shy and nervous, she felt a new sense of confidence. That day marked the beginning of a sweet, innocent connection between them—a bond that would grow as they got to know each other.

Months had passed, and Sam came over frequently. Jake refused to let Sam see Christy, believing he was protecting her. Little did he know, Christy and Sam were facing a serious situation. They had to make a difficult decision: stay and face Jake's anger, or run away together. They chose to run away.

After twenty-four hours, Jake contacted the police and filed a missing persons report. Christy's picture was broadcast on television. Sam and Christy thought they were safe, but they hadn't anticipated being recognized. The bus driver who had taken them to West Virginia saw her picture on TV and called the number they had provided, revealing their destination.

When Sam and Christy got off the bus, they were met by the police, along with Jake and his brother Tom. The couple wanted to run, but there was nowhere to go. One officer approached Christy, took her arm, and led her over to where her father was standing. Another officer placed handcuffs on Sam.

Officer Collins asked Jake if he wanted to press charges, explaining that Sam could potentially face two counts. Jake shook his head, choosing a different approach to handle the situation.

Christy was only sixteen years old. Jake told the officer no. He had a better idea. So the officer turned Sam over to Jake and Tom and they headed home. On the way home Jake told Sam he was going to hang him from an oak tree when he found one big enough, he even had a bull rope with a noose on it, in the back of the station wagon, but of course he never used it.

They made it home after hours on the road. Sam and Christy hadn't realized they had traveled that far—they only went as far as their money would take them. Now back home, they had to face Jake and Ellan and tell them the news: Christy was going to have a baby.

It was late, and the house was quiet; everyone else was in bed. Tom stayed up, having coffee and a sandwich, partly to keep an eye on Jake and make sure he didn't react too harshly.

When the news was finally out, Jake took it surprisingly lightly. However, he insisted that there would be a wedding and told Sam that he would work with him until they had enough money to start their own life with the baby.

They lived together and got married, with Christy now four months into her pregnancy. Tragically, at six months, the baby was stillborn.

Christy was in a state of depression. The loss of the baby weighed heavily on her, and she somehow felt responsible. She had to come to terms with herself and learn to accept God's mysterious ways. She moped around all day, thinking about the little baby girl, with far too much time on her hands.

Sam decided to work longer hours so they could save enough to get their own place. He reasoned that with a home to take care of, Christy wouldn't have so much idle time to dwell on her sorrow. He was right. They found a small, three-room apartment in town—a warm and cozy little place.

Christy kept herself busy fixing up the apartment, cleaning the walls, scrubbing the carpets, hanging curtains, and preparing everything for their move-in. By the time they were settled, she was feeling much better.

However, the voices had returned. They kept calling her name. When she answered, all they did was call again, as if urging her to follow them. But Christy chose to ignore them, just as her grandmother had advised.

After a few weeks, Christy had the apartment all fixed up. Now there were too many hours in the day. She finally had time to relax and think—but this was not good for her. *Her problem started again.*

She leaned back, breathed deeply, and felt her mind begin to drift. A gentle motion rocked her back and forth. She felt woozy. Slowly, images formed in her mind: she saw herself in another place, a large room filled with many people—young and old, couples with children. Some were talking excitedly about the new world and what their lives might be like there. Others were terrified by what awaited them at the end of their journey. The motion must be a ship, sailing across the ocean to America.

Christy didn't recognize the people around her. She knew they were not from the present day. Their clothing was distinctly old-world: women wore long skirts and bonnets, boys had knickers, and the men wore round-rimmed hats with heavy wool jackets. Christy suspected they might be from Ireland or Scotland. Slowly, she scanned the vessel. It looked ancient, possibly late eighteenth century, with massive wooden beams. The area the people occupied resembled a cargo hold rather than a passenger deck.

Christy was very confused by all of this. *She feels like the person sitting there.* She could smell the salt water in the air and feel every motion as the waves struck the side of the ship. The air in the cargo hold was foul, heavy with the stench of people who had been at sea for a very long time. Some of the passengers looked as if they were starving. Their clothes were filthy, their bodies exhausted. The children were restless, and tension hung thick in the air. Everyone seemed upset about something.

Christy didn't understand what was happening, but she knew something was terribly wrong. *But what?* she wondered.

Suddenly, the ship rolled violently from side to side. Christy felt the panic rising within her. She had to know what was going on. In the far corner of the room, she spotted a pail of water. She walked over and peered into it.

The reflection she saw startled her. Looking back at her from the water was the image of a young man, maybe in his early twenties, with dark hair and piercing grey eyes. Now she was even more confused—she saw what he saw, felt what he felt. *How could this be?* she thought. It was impossible. Then she realized, somehow, she had become this young man. But why?

Christy tried to pull herself back to reality, but she couldn't. She was locked into this life. Panic surged through her, and she understood that the young man was panicking too.

The ship rolled again on its side, tossed violently by the sea. A terrible storm raged: loud thunder, blinding flashes of lightning, and water pouring over the bow and into the portholes. The vessel pitched back and forth, again and again. People were thrown around like dolls, screaming, clutching anything they could hold.

A woman screamed, "My God, we're all going to die!" Children clung to their parents. Old men and their wives knelt to pray, and babies cried as their mothers tried to reassure them that everything would be okay. One woman sang softly to her baby, trying to calm them. *This is horrible.*

On the deck, men screamed orders to the sailors, trying desperately to manage the ship in the storm. Water poured in everywhere. Terror filled every corner. Men and women huddled together, trying to protect their loved ones from this dreadful fate. Screaming echoed all around. Everyone was in sheer panic.

The ship rolled again, deeper this time. Waves crashed violently against the deck. It tipped back the other way. The young man knew they were going to die. He prayed, asking the Lord to have mercy on their souls. Water surged in, and people scrambled, trying to reach the surface. One woman was thrown against a wall, breaking her neck. The baby in her arms was cast into the water.

The young man dove after the child. Swimming to the surface, he held the baby in one arm. He looked around and saw trunks and wooden boxes floating nearby, with rats and mice clinging desperately for survival. But it was impossible— there was too much water. The compartment was nearly full, and air was scarce. People were drowning all around him.

He fought to stay afloat, gripping the baby tightly. Each dive pushed him deeper. His chest ached, lungs burned, and he swallowed water. Gasping, he came up again, only to find no air. Still, he battled on, knowing the sea was swallowing him and all the passengers.

Christy jolted back to reality. She gasped for air, her lungs aching as if they were tearing apart. Fear gripped her. She didn't understand how or why she had experienced it, only that she was alive—and had once again glimpsed the "face of death."

She kept her secret to herself. Afraid others might think her insane, she carried the burden alone. To cope, she filled her days with constant activity. From morning until night, she worked herself to exhaustion, leaving no room to relax and slip away into the visions.

Sleeping was different—it allowed her mind to rest without opening the door to the visions. To stay busy, she cleaned the apartment, helped the landlord with yard work, and tackled any task she could find. This routine, though exhausting, was the only way she and Sam could find peace in their new home.

CHAPTER
Four

No More Secrets

$\mathcal{S}$oon Christy became pregnant. They were both delighted about the baby, but Christy worried about the possibility of losing this one too. Months went by, and everything seemed to be going well. The doctor said the baby was very healthy and growing at a normal rate. Christy was relieved—but she still had other worries.

Sam was acting strangely. Everyone told Christy it was just because she was pregnant and feeling "fat and sloppy," that all women go through these phases when they're expecting. But Christy knew better—her instincts were right. Sam was having an affair with a young girl who lived just down the street. At the time, Christy didn't know this for sure. She only sensed that something was different. Call it women's intuition.

One day, while Christy was cleaning the apartment, she felt a sharp pain. At first, she thought it was just cramps. But shortly after, another pain hit. She called her mother, Ellan, and explained what was happening. Ellan told her to time the pains. Then she asked if Christy knew how to get in touch with Sam. Christy replied, "No, Mom, I don't. He's out on a job, and they don't have a phone there."

What Christy didn't know was that it wouldn't have mattered—Sam wasn't at work anyway. He had taken the day off to go swimming with his girlfriend. Ellan told Christy not to worry about Sam and reassured her, "Your dad and I will be right over." She hung up, called Christy's landlord, and explained the situation. The landlord promised to stay with Christy until they arrived.

Ellan and Jake set out immediately. Even so, it took them about twenty minutes to reach Christy's apartment. By the time they arrived, Christy had already contacted her doctor. He told her he would be waiting at the hospital and instructed her not to waste any time. On the way there, Christy's water broke.

At the hospital, the doctor examined her. She wasn't yet dilated enough, so he gave her medication to help move labor along. Christy endured almost twenty hours of labor, the last two in very hard labor. She was terrified, fearing something might be wrong with the baby—and with good reason. She had no experience and had already lost one baby.

Finally, she gave birth to a boy—a beautiful baby with blonde hair and blue eyes. All the nurses raved over him, marveling at his light hair. They spoiled him rotten even before Christy could take him home.

While Christy was in the hospital, Sam visited infrequently. He explained he was working long hours to cover the extra bills that came with a baby. Christy understood. She did the shopping and managed the household finances, so she knew how important Sam's earnings were.

Christy and the baby stayed in the hospital for four days. The doctor checked them both and cleared them to go home. Sam picked them up, and Christy was thrilled to take her new baby home. She discovered that he was not only beautiful but an easy baby. He rarely cried, as long as he was fed and changed, and Christy felt confident that she was doing a good job as a new mother.

The apartment felt warm and cozy to Christy when she got home. It felt good to be home. Life was starting to feel manageable, and she kept herself busy with the baby, so she hardly had time to think about anything else. Sam went off to work every day like clockwork.

After a few weeks, Sam came home one Friday evening. Christy was waiting for him—payday—and she needed to go to the store for milk and cereal for the baby. She asked Sam if he had been paid, and he said no, making up the lame excuse that the boss hadn't come to the job that day. He lied, of course, but Christy had no idea. She asked him, "What will we do? The baby needs milk."

Sam told her to call her mother and father and borrow the money. She did, and Jake asked what she needed and promised to bring it right over. But he didn't do it for Sam—he did it for Christy and the baby. Jake was very angry with Sam. He knew something was wrong; Sam had been gone so many hours for such little money. But Jake didn't confront him—he didn't want to upset Christy, and he figured the truth would come out sooner or later. And it did.

Come Monday morning, Sam was supposed to go to work. Christy asked him why he hadn't gone, and he snapped, "It's none of your business." "It is my business," she replied, "I'm your wife." Sam got angry. He pulled back his arm and punched her. When Christy tried to defend herself, it angered him more, and he hit her again, sending her to the floor. Her nose was bleeding, but Sam didn't care.

He ran out the door and was gone all day, returning late at night, drunk and sloppy. Christy asked him where he had been, but he didn't answer. Instead, he came at her in a rage.

He punched her again, and this time she fell over a kitchen chair, hurting her arm, but she got back to her feet. Sam struck her once more, hitting her across the nose, blood squirting everywhere. Christy tried to escape, but he followed her. She tried to reach the bedroom to check on the baby, but Sam blocked her.

"Where are you going?" he demanded.

"I thought I heard the baby cry," she said.

Sam called her a lying bitch and hit her again, waking the baby. Christy tried to get to him, but Sam wouldn't let her. The noise roused the landlord, who at first had no idea what was happening. As she listened, she realized something was terribly wrong. Sam had knocked Christy to the floor, and she lay there crying, afraid to move. Every time she tried, he kicked her. He had kicked her several times. Her ribs ached with every breath, and her whole body throbbed with pain.

Finally, the landlord banged on the door. Sam hovered over Christy like an animal over its prey, refusing to open it. The landlord pounded harder, but he still wouldn't answer. "Mind your own business!" he screamed. "Leave us alone!" The landlord feared for Christy's life. She went home and called the police. After hanging up, she called Jake and Ellan.

"I'm so sorry to bother you at this late hour," she said, "but Christy needs your help." She explained what she knew. Jake told her they would be right there and hung up. The landlord set the phone down, unsure what else to do. She decided to go out on the porch to wait for the police.

The police arrived, and Jake pulled up right after them. The officer in charge asked Jake to stay back while they went into the apartment to check on Christy. Jake agreed and let the police do their job.

Once the door was opened, they saw Christy lying on the floor. Sam ran toward the bedroom window, attempting to escape, but the police caught him just as he tried to climb through. They handcuffed him and took him into custody. Sam put up a fight, struggling against the cuffs and even hitting an officer. With no other choice, they arrested him.

Christy remained on the floor when her mom and dad entered the apartment. They checked her carefully, then helped her to the bed. Jake wanted to take Christy to the hospital, but she refused, saying she would be okay now that Sam was gone.

The landlord stayed until she was sure Christy was safe. Over time, the landlord and Christy had grown very close. Their friendship developed gradually, mostly after Sam began spending long hours away from home. Christy spent a lot of time alone and had no one to talk to, so she started visiting her landlord, and eventually, they became very good friends.

The landlady, Maria, was a short, husky Italian woman. She seemed to take Christy under her wing, and Christy came to love her almost like a second mother. Maria loved helping with the baby, especially during bath time, treating him as if he were her own grandchild. Before Christy moved in, Maria's life had been lonely. Her husband had passed away just before Sam and Christy moved into the apartment, and she had no family. Their friendship fulfilled a deep need for both of them—they found comfort and companionship in each other during times of sorrow and despair.

Jake went into the kitchen to make some coffee while Ellan stayed in the bedroom with Christy and the baby, rocking him gently to keep him quiet. Ellan and Christy talked about everything that had been happening with Sam. Meanwhile, Maria and Jake sat at the kitchen table, discussing the situation in private.

After a while, Jake left the kitchen and went to the bedroom. He sat slowly on the edge of the bed, deep in thought for a few minutes. Then he reached for his daughter's hand and said, "Christy, you can't go on living like this. If you don't do something about this mess, you might end up dead the next time. And there will be a next time. People like Sam don't just change—they get worse. I'm afraid for your safety and the baby's."

He continued, "You have to make a choice. You simply can't live like this."

Christy looked up at her father. "Dad, I've been thinking about leaving for some time, but I didn't know what to do or where to go. How could I live and take care of the baby? I have no money."

Jake reassured her. "You can make it if you put your mind to it."

Christy asked if she and the baby could come home temporarily until she got a job and saved enough money for a place of her own. Jake told her she could stay as long as she needed to get her life together.

Shortly afterward, Christy and Ellan began packing. They prepared everything so it would be ready for the next day when they brought the truck. Christy gathered all the essentials for herself and the baby so they could move in comfortably. The very next day, Christy and the baby moved back home with her mom and dad.

Sam, being in jail, had some time to sober up. That also meant he had plenty of time to think about what he had done. He was allowed one telephone call, and of course, he tried to call Christy. She wasn't home, so he dialed Jake's number instead. Christy answered the phone and was stunned to hear Sam's voice on the line.

He started by apologizing, but Christy knew better—this wasn't the first time. Sam pleaded with her to come and get him out of jail. Calmly, Christy said, "No. You deserve to be there. You hit me and kicked me. You wanted to kill me. You are the one in the wrong, not me. I will not take another beating from you—or from any man. I'm finished with you."

Sam cried and begged, but Christy could tell it was all for show. He had done this before, trying to manipulate her. This time, it didn't work. "Sorry, Sam. I'm leaving," she said, and hung up.

Knowing Christy wasn't going to help, Sam called some of his family for assistance. By the time they got him out of jail, Christy had already packed and left the apartment. She had gathered everything she needed and said her goodbyes to Maria. Maria was heartbroken—she would miss Christy and the baby terribly. Christy hugged her tightly and reassured her, "We'll be okay. Tomorrow, I'm starting a new life for myself and my baby."

Christy wasn't entirely happy about the situation, but she knew in her heart it was the right thing to do. Sam, on the other hand, was reveling in his freedom. Since leaving jail, he had been drinking and chasing after women, caring only about himself.

About a week later, Christy went to the store and ran into Sam's old boss. He asked how she and the baby were doing. She smiled and said they were fine—and that she felt relieved to be free from Sam. Now she didn't have to endure any more beatings.

They stood in the aisle talking for a while. Sam's boss told her she was better off where she was. He admitted that Sam had been cheating on her for some time and had even brought women to work to pick up his paychecks. He explained that he had wanted to tell her sooner but didn't know how without hurting her further.

"I'm sorry, Christy," he said. "You deserve better. Sam is a bum. He only thinks about what he wants. You and your baby are not part of that."

He shook her hand warmly. "Get on with your life. You're a beautiful young woman, and there's a whole world out there.

All you have to do is reach for it. Don't waste your life on Sam—he'll only hold you back."

Christy finished her shopping, thinking about what he had said. At that moment, she made a decision: she would build a better life for herself and her son.

Christy found a job almost immediately, and Ellan took care of the baby while Christy worked. After a few months, she had earned enough money to apply for a divorce from Sam. Determined to improve her life, she went back to school in the evenings and earned her diploma.

A year later, Christy felt proud of herself. Everything seemed to be falling into place. She was supporting herself and her son and was finally ready to look for a place of her own. She found a small house near the diner where she worked. It was affordable, convenient, and perfectly located for her job.

Marion, her boss, helped as much as she could. She had grown fond of Christy and felt protective of her. A young woman, divorced and raising a child on her own, was not an easy life, and Marion wanted to make it a little safer for her. She welcomed Christy into her life and treated her like one of her own daughters. Marion's husband shared her affection for Christy and loved the baby as well. They both enjoyed having a child around and looked forward to becoming grandparents someday.

At this point in her life, everything was good for Christy. She was rich in ways that money could not measure—friends, family, and people who cared deeply about her and her child surrounded her. On top of that, she had a very good job. The pay was decent, and she earned excellent tips. Everyone had believed she would do well at her job—and she did.

Still, Christy harbored a quiet hope in her heart. She was successful, independent, and well-loved—but she still dreamed of finding Mr. Right.

Christy had been working for Marion at the diner for about a year and a half. One afternoon, right after the lunch-hour rush, one of the most handsome men Christy had ever seen came through the door. He slid onto a stool at the end of the snack bar.

Christy grabbed a menu and made her way over. When she reached him, she handed it to him and said, "Hello. Can I get you something to drink?"

The stranger asked, "How's the coffee?"

Christy replied, "It's fine, but not quite finished yet. It'll be a couple of minutes, but at least it'll be fresh."

He asked, "Did you make it?"

"Yes," she said.

He smiled and said, "I'd wait all day for coffee made by your own hands," winking at her as she turned to get it. Christy blushed and giggled to herself.

She poured him some coffee and returned to take his order. When she heard what he wanted, she was slightly overwhelmed—he didn't look like someone who could eat that much, but when the food arrived, he ate every bite. Then he asked, "What's for dessert?"

All the while, he never took his eyes off Christy. At first, she felt nervous under his gaze, but gradually, she began to enjoy it. After he finished dessert, Christy asked if he wanted anything else.

"Yes," he said, "in a doggie bag."

Christy's face turned bright red. Their eyes met, and she felt her whole body trembling. *Oh God,* she thought, *I must look like some silly schoolgirl.* She hadn't felt this way in a long time.

The stranger paid his bill, leaving a very generous tip. On the back of the receipt, he wrote:

"A pleasure meeting you. I will be back. Love, Gene."

As he left, the other girls at the diner teased Christy about her admirer. One of them even knew him. She told Christy that Gene was a construction worker who traveled a lot. She had known him from when he went to school with her brother. When he wasn't away, he worked on his family farm, helping raise beef cattle and horses. They also trained horses for rodeo competitions.

About a week later, Gene came back to the diner—this time on crutches. It seemed that while training a horse, he had been thrown off and hit a split-rail fence, breaking his leg in two places. But despite the injury, he simply couldn't stay away. He needed to see Christy again and again. As soon as he was able, he returned to the diner.

After a few visits, he felt he knew her well enough to ask her out—and Christy accepted. By then, Gene had healed enough to take her to dinner and dancing. They chose Saturday for their date.

When Saturday came, Christy was so nervous she could hardly do anything right. She hadn't been on a date since her divorce, and Sam had been the only man she'd ever been with. Nevertheless, by seven o'clock she was ready, dressed to the nines.

The babysitter arrived on time, and when Gene showed up, they were all set to go. They had one of the most beautiful dates Christy could have imagined. They started at the finest restaurant in the area. After dinner, they drove to the next town, where a tavern featured a country-western band. They danced until the music stopped, then danced to the jukebox until they were practically thrown out. Realizing it was late, they decided to go home before Christy's mother sent out a search party.

Christy had a wonderful time, and Gene was the perfect gentleman. He talked about his family and his life and asked Christy if she would visit his parents' farm the following weekend. She happily agreed. After spending a little more time together over coffee, Gene said he had to leave—he had a lot of work the next morning. They kissed goodnight, and he went home, feeling on cloud nine. He couldn't stop thinking about Christy and the fantastic time they had shared.

For the next few days, Gene talked about nothing else. His family grew tired of hearing about her and asked when they would finally meet her, just to see what he was raving about. They teased him, saying he was like a lovesick puppy, but were happy that he had found someone he cared for. Gene had always feared being hurt, but that didn't matter anymore. He was willing to take a chance on Christy—she was a wonderful woman, and he was in love.

Finally, the next weekend arrived, and they went to the farm to meet Gene's parents. It quickly became clear why Gene had fallen in love. His parents adored Christy, and his mother and Christy hit it off immediately, spending hours in the kitchen cooking, talking, and laughing. Gene felt reassured— the day had gone perfectly.

After that visit, Gene and Christy saw each other every day. About three months later, Gene moved in with Christy. Soon after, Christy became pregnant, and they were both thrilled. Christy was confident that Gene would be a wonderful father. He adored Sammie Jr., taking him everywhere, playing ball, and wrestling with him whenever he had the chance. His dedication to the child made Christy feel secure in their relationship and brought them even closer together.

Life was going very well, and then things got even better. Gene asked Christy to marry him, and of course, she happily accepted. Everyone was thrilled about the proposal, and with family and friends pulling together, they began planning a beautiful wedding.

Over the next six weeks, both families worked tirelessly, along with Marion and her staff, to make everything perfect. Gene's family, Christy's family, and Marion's team all pitched in, knowing they had to move fast so Gene could make an honest woman of Christy. When the preparations were complete, they had a stunning country wedding at Gene's parents' farm. There was plenty of room for everyone to spread out and enjoy themselves.

What had started as a small, intimate ceremony turned into quite the celebration—half the town seemed to attend! Both Gene and Christy were well-liked, with many friends and acquaintances eager to celebrate with them. There was no drama, no fighting, just a lot of laughter, dancing, and good old-fashioned fun.

Gene and Christy decided not to go on a traditional honeymoon. Instead, everyone involved in the wedding fixed up a small bungalow behind the main house for the newlyweds. They called it the "honeymoon suite" and, of course, included all the classic playful pranks. They short-sheeted the bed, filled the showerhead with lime Jell-O so the water ran green, and added a few profane—but all in good fun—jokes, knowing the couple had a good sense of humor.

The newlyweds tried to sneak away in the dark, hoping for a quiet, private moment. But things didn't go exactly as planned. Halfway down the path to the bungalow, Christy slipped on wet grass. Gene fell on top of her as he tried to break her fall. They tumbled and rolled in the grass, laughing uncontrollably. When they got back up and continued down the path, Gene tripped, and Christy, holding onto him, fell too. They rolled again, giggling, teasing each other—but before long, the moment became more serious.

Gene kissed Christy, telling her she looked beautiful in the moonlight. The kiss deepened, growing more passionate, and soon they were lost in each other. In the moonlight, they felt like the only two people in the world. Though they had made love before, this time it felt different—more intimate, more sacred, as if their marriage had changed everything. They cherished the moment fully.

Their passion was interrupted, however, by voices approaching down the path. Gene scrambled to pull up his pants, and Christy quickly got her gown back in place. Seeing her undergarments on the ground, she pressed them to her chest and quietly handed them to Gene, who slipped them into his pocket. The voices belonged to some of the young wedding guests, who were on their way to the bungalow. Gene grinned and told Christy, "Not a chance—that's where we're going, and we don't need company. We know what to do."

The young guests laughed and went back to the party, leaving Gene and Christy to finally enjoy their private moment, savoring the joy, laughter, and love that surrounded them.

What Gene and Christy didn't know was that someone had a few more tricks up their sleeve for the honeymoon suite. But the newlyweds had a treat awaiting them anyway. They finally made it to the bungalow, and Gene carried Christy over the threshold.

"Welcome to my humble cabin," he said. Then he told her how much time he had spent there growing up. "I've always loved this place," he said. "It feels like it's in a world all its own, separate from everyone else. When I needed time to be alone, this was it." He chuckled as he added, "I used to pretend I was Daniel Boone, and my sister pretended to be Annie Oakley. We had the best times playing out here. Mom and Dad always knew where to find us when they needed to."

They talked for hours, sharing stories until the early morning, before finally making love again and falling asleep in each other's arms.

The next day, around noon, they both woke up and headed for the shower, racing to see who would get there first. They arrived at the same time, wrestled for a bit, and realized there was no clear winner. Finally, they decided there was only one way to settle it—they would shower together.

They stepped in, turned on the water, and became completely absorbed in each other. Suddenly, Gene stopped kissing Christy and noticed the water running green. Both of them jumped out of the shower in shock, then burst into laughter as they realized someone had played a prank on them.

"You've got to hand it to whoever did this," Gene said between laughs. "It worked!"

They looked at each other in the mirror, completely naked, covered in green slime, and laughed even harder. "We can't get dressed like this!" Christy exclaimed. They turned off the shower and began cleaning the sticky lime Jell-O off their bodies. It took several rinses to get most of it off, though a few stubborn patches remained—but they could easily hide those with clothes.

Afterwards, they laughed about the prank, knowing it was their little secret. Soon it was time for breakfast. They ate, then headed down to the creek, lying on the bank in the warm sun and talking for hours.

Gene shared stories about life on the farm and his childhood adventures. Then it was Christy's turn. She opened up, telling him about her upbringing—and eventually, all of her secrets. She spoke about the extraordinary experiences she had lived through. When she finished, she nervously asked, "Do you think I'm crazy?"

Gene smiled and said, "I love to read, and I've read a book about things like this. It says this kind of thing happens to a lot of people—but most of them get hypnotized or manipulated into it. You're not crazy. You're extraordinary."

Christy looked very sad, and Gene held her close, trying to reassure her. "You're not a freak of nature," he said gently. "You're extraordinary, that's all."

After a long pause, Gene asked, "Christy... how do you do it? How do these... experiences happen?"

She took a deep breath, tears welling up in her eyes. "I don't know exactly," she admitted. "It's weird… I just sit, relax, breathe deeply, and concentrate for a little while. Then the pictures start to appear in my head. And before I know it, I drift right into them. I become the person in the picture— the one everything happens to. I feel what they feel, see what they see, and live what they live. Their entire life becomes mine. Their families, the places they live, their work… it's like I leave this life and step into another one, without knowing how. Sometimes it scares me so badly that I just sit and cry. I feel their pain, even as they die. I am that person. I am the one who actually dies."

Her voice shook as she spoke, and more tears fell. Gene held her tightly, stroking her hair and whispering that she would be okay.

Then Christy hesitated, her expression darkening. "There's more," she said softly.

Gene tilted his head. "More? What do you mean?"

Christy poured out her heart. She told him about the voices—the ones that called her name. How frightened she was of them. "They want me to follow them," she said, her hands trembling. "I… I did, a couple of times, and I almost died. But something… something always saved me, right at the last moment."

Gene listened, bewildered, his brow furrowed. "Honey… why do you think they want to hurt you?"

"They're not… human," Christy whispered. "They want to destroy me. I don't know why, but they do."

Gene held her even closer, his mind racing to make sense of what she was saying. "Okay," he said softly. "Take it easy. Try not to think about it for now. Just breathe. I'm right here, and you're safe."

Christy leaned into him, letting herself be held. For the first time in a long while, she felt a small measure of peace.

Gene and Christy returned to the bungalow for dinner. While Christy was busy cooking, Gene excused himself and went to the big house, promising he'd be right back.

Almost as soon as he left, Christy heard them—the voices. Soft at first, calling her name, then growing more insistent. *"Christy… come to me… I'm right outside."*

She froze, her heart pounding, but she ignored them. By now, she was getting used to the voices, but they seemed to be growing more demanding, more forceful. They didn't like being ignored, but Christy had no choice. The fear they instilled was too strong; she couldn't let herself respond. She truly believed they wanted to harm her. Determined not to succumb, she threw herself into her cooking, keeping busy until Gene returned.

A short while later, Gene came running through the door, holding a book. "Here," he said, handing it to her. "Read this. It might help you feel better." He hugged her tightly, smiled, and whispered, "You're not crazy. I love you very much. Even if you grew a big, ugly nose and turned green, I'd still love you."

Christy tucked the book into her purse and read it at every opportunity. She made the time because she knew that understanding what was happening to her could make all the difference.

By the end of the honeymoon, she had finished the book. It was helpful, teaching her how to control her drifting—how to enter these other lives and, more importantly, how to return if she felt uncomfortable or in danger.

Still, the book didn't answer everything. Most importantly, it said nothing about the voices. Christy's curiosity—and her fear—remained. *"They're evil,"* she thought, shivering at the memory of their demands. She considered asking Gene about them, then smiled to herself. *Isn't it funny? He got some of my answers from a book. Why didn't I think of that?*

With that thought, she returned to her chores, determined to face both her work and the mystery of her gift—one step at a time.

Married life was good for Gene and Christy. They decided to live in Christy's house for a while, so she wouldn't be alone while Gene traveled from job to job. He promised her that it wouldn't last forever—he would change jobs as soon as he could. Until then, life required some adjustment. Gene still helped out on his parents' farm on the weekends, so they spent their weekends at the farm, staying in the bungalow. They could have lived there permanently, but that would have made Christy's commute to the diner inconvenient.

Besides, Sammie Jr. loved the farm. It gave him something to look forward to at the end of the week, and Gene's parents, who had no other grandchildren, adored him like he was their very own. Sammie even called Gene's father "Pops." Pops spent hours with him, taking him down to the creek to catch tadpoles and crabs, letting him ride on the tractor, and exploring the hay fields together. He even let Sammie pretend to drive the tractor and gave him his own little pony. The farm life was good for Sammie, and it gave Christy peace of mind as well. She was in her eighth month of pregnancy and working only part-time at the diner. She had to be careful not to go into labor early, and after a previous scare, she followed the doctor's strict instructions closely.

At the diner, Marion missed Christy terribly. Christy was one of her best workers—efficient, attentive, and personable. Every customer felt like they were the only one in the diner when Christy waited on them. With Christy working part-time, Marion had to manage things carefully, but she still spent a lot of time with Christy and Sammie. She loved the little boy and spoiled him endlessly, always bringing little treats whenever she came into town. Sammie knew when Marion arrived, a surprise awaited him in the car.

Marion often told Christy she couldn't wait for the new baby to arrive so she could spoil it too. Christy cherished Marion's company. They went to lunch together, took Sammie to the park, and spent hours talking. These days, Christy needed to keep her mind busy, and Marion's friendship was a perfect comfort.

CHAPTER
Five

A Face In The Water

Christy tried to keep herself very busy these days. When they weren't at the farm or the bungalow, they spent time at Jake and Ellan's house. Jake really liked his new son-in-law, Gene, and they spent a lot of time together whenever Gene had free time. They shared many interests, particularly a love for horses and farming. Jake even went out to Gene's parents' farm when they began breaking horses for competition. Although Jake wasn't as young as he used to be, he was still impressive with the horses—skills like that, once mastered, never truly fade. Gene's father enjoyed having Jake around; they were about the same age and liked reminiscing about the "good old days." Over time, the two men became not only in-laws but very good friends. While the men were together, Christy enjoyed spending quality time with her mother.

Ellan had been very sick lately. Doctors ran many tests but couldn't find a conclusive answer. The pain she experienced was real, however. It struck her suddenly, causing her to double over in agony, centered behind her right ribs and along her lower right side. She would feel very ill when the pain hit. One day, Christy was with her when it worsened, and they rushed Ellan to the hospital. There, the doctors discovered kidney stones lodged in the upper part of her right kidney. The surgery was dangerous; they had to open the kidney to remove the stones and scrape the inside to ensure it was completely cleared.

After the operation, Ellan remained very ill. An infection set in, and at one point, the doctors feared for her life. But Ellan, being a tough woman, pulled through. "The Lord isn't finished with me yet," she said, and soon enough, she was back on her feet. Christy helped as much as she could, though she was in the final month of her pregnancy and had her own health to consider.

A week later, Ellan had grown accustomed to Christy and Sammie's presence, missing them terribly. They spent quiet afternoons together, talking and enjoying each other's company. One afternoon, while they were relaxing in the backyard, Christy felt her first labor pain. Ellan screamed for Christy's sister to come help, and together they got her inside. Moments later, Christy's water broke. Ellan quickly called Gene, and Christy was rushed to the hospital. After a short while, she gave birth to a beautiful little girl. Like her brother, she had blonde hair, blue eyes, and was perfectly healthy.

After a three-day stay in the hospital, Gene took Christy and the new baby home. He had arranged a week off from work to help out until Christy regained her strength. The days went smoothly, with Christy adjusting to life with two children and the baby settling in nicely.

Soon, it was time for Gene to return to work. He kissed Christy and the children goodbye, promising he would be back soon. While he was on the job, he couldn't help but think of home. He felt proud of his growing family and eagerly anticipated returning to them each evening. Gene was grateful for his new job, as it allowed him to provide for his family while still being present for the moments that mattered most.

Gene stayed by Christy's side, holding her tightly as she tried to steady her breathing. Her hands were clammy, and her body trembled as if she'd run a marathon. He could see the fear in her eyes and knew this was more than exhaustion or stress—something was truly troubling her.

"Christy," he said softly, brushing a strand of hair from her face, "we're going to figure this out. You're not alone in this, okay? I'm right here with you."

Christy clung to him, her voice barely a whisper. "It's the voices, Gene… they won't leave me alone. They're… they're demanding things, making me feel… like I'm not safe anywhere."

Gene's mind raced. He didn't understand how or why this was happening, but he knew one thing: he had to protect her and their children. "We'll get through this together," he said firmly. "Whatever this is, we'll face it. I promise you."

For a long while, they sat there in silence. The house was quiet except for the faint hum of the heater and the distant sounds of the children playing. Gradually, Christy's trembling slowed, and her breathing became more regular. Gene kept his arms wrapped around her, not letting go even as she started to relax.

"Do you think… I'm crazy?" Christy asked after a while, her voice small and uncertain.

Gene shook his head, a determined look on his face. "No, Christy. You are not crazy. Something is happening, yes… but that doesn't make you insane. We'll find out what it is, and we'll get you through it. I swear it."

Christy rested her head against his chest, feeling some comfort in his words. She didn't fully understand what was happening to her, but for the first time in a long while, she felt a glimmer of hope.

And outside, the night was quiet, but somewhere in the shadows, the voices whispered still, waiting for their next move.

Christy leaned into Gene, her body shaking as she cried softly. She felt the safety of his arms around her, the warmth of his embrace easing just a little of the fear that had haunted her for so long.

"I... I don't know if I can do it," she whispered. "What if they don't understand? What if they think I'm making it up?"

Gene cupped her face in his hands, looking into her eyes with unwavering determination. "Christy, listen to me. Your parents love you. They've always loved you. And I love you. None of us think you're crazy. You're my wife, the mother of our children, and you've been through more than anyone should have to face alone. It's time we share this burden. We face it together."

Christy sniffled and nodded weakly. "Okay... but what if the voices come back while they're here?"

Gene smiled gently. "Then we'll face that too. I'll be right here with you. And we'll figure out what's really happening. I promise."

She took a deep breath, trying to steady her racing heart. "Okay... let's call them."

Gene picked up the phone again and dialed Jake's number. Within minutes, Jake and Ellan arrived, bringing Sammie with them, who ran straight to Christy and hugged her tightly. Seeing the comfort in her parents' faces gave Christy the courage to speak.

Once they were all seated, Gene took Christy's hand and said, "Christy has something important she needs to tell you. Something she's been dealing with her whole life, and she hasn't been able to share it until now."

Christy swallowed hard, her hands trembling as she began to tell the story. She recounted the voices, the trances, the fear, and the experiences that had haunted her since childhood. She told them about the creek, the mud, and the panic of those early moments. She even admitted how the voices had returned recently, stronger and more demanding than ever.

Jake and Ellan listened quietly, exchanging glances but saying nothing. When Christy finished, her voice barely audible, the room was silent for a long moment.

Finally, Jake reached across the table, taking her hands in his. "Christy… you're not crazy. We don't think that. We just… we didn't know, and we wish you'd told us sooner. But we're here now. We'll help you through this, whatever it takes."

Ellan nodded, tears in her eyes. "You're our daughter. We love you, and we'll do everything we can to protect you and the children. You don't have to carry this alone anymore."

Christy felt a wave of relief wash over her. For the first time in her life, she felt truly understood, truly supported. And with Gene holding her close, and her parents by her side, she realized she might finally have the strength to confront the voices, to face them head-on, and maybe—just maybe—find peace.

The next morning, Christy woke early, still feeling nervous about seeing a doctor. Gene was already up, making breakfast and keeping Sammie and the baby entertained. He smiled at Christy when she entered the kitchen. "Good morning, beautiful. Ready for today?"

Christy hesitated, stirring her coffee slowly. "I guess so… I just… I don't know what to expect. What if the doctor thinks I'm… crazy?"

Gene walked over and wrapped his arms around her from behind, resting his chin on her shoulder. "Christy, you're not crazy. You're brave. That's all that matters. And whatever happens, we'll face it together. I'll be there every step of the way."

Christy gave a small, shaky smile. "Okay... I trust you."

After breakfast, Jake and Ellan arrived to drive Christy to the appointment. Sammie and the baby waved goodbye as Christy left with her parents. The drive was quiet at first, Christy lost in thought, trying to calm her racing mind.

Jake broke the silence gently. "Christy... I just want you to know, whatever the doctor says, we love you. Nothing can change that. You're our daughter, and we'll always be here for you."

Ellan nodded, reaching over to squeeze Christy's hand. "And we're proud of you for doing this. It's not easy, but it's the right thing. You're not alone anymore, honey."

Christy took a deep breath, tears welling in her eyes. "Thanks... I... I really needed to hear that."

When they arrived at the clinic, Christy felt a mixture of fear and relief. The receptionist led her to a quiet room, and soon the doctor arrived—a calm, understanding woman who made Christy feel immediately at ease. After listening patiently, asking questions, and reviewing Christy's history, the doctor said, "Christy, what you've been experiencing is very real, and you are not alone in this. There are ways we can help you understand these episodes and learn to manage them safely. You did the right thing by coming today."

Christy felt a wave of relief wash over her. For the first time in her life, someone believed her without hesitation. She looked at Jake, Ellan, and Gene, who all smiled reassuringly, and for the first time, she felt hope instead of fear.

The doctor continued, explaining options for therapy, grounding techniques, and ways to track and manage the episodes. Christy listened intently, scribbling notes in her notebook. She realized that, with support, she could regain control over her life.

As they left the clinic, Christy felt lighter than she had in years. Gene wrapped his arm around her shoulders, pulling her close. "See? Nothing can stop us now. You've taken the first step, Christy. And we're all here for you."

Christy looked up at him, a small smile forming on her lips. "Yeah… I think… I think I can do this."

And for the first time in a very long time, she truly believed it.

By the time the weekend arrived, Christy felt a mixture of nervous anticipation and cautious optimism. She hadn't experienced anything unusual for days, and that gave her a small sense of relief. But deep down, she knew better than to let herself relax completely. The voices could return at any moment, and when they did, there would be no warning.

Ellan kept Christy busy in the kitchen, trying new recipes and baking treats for the grandchildren. Sammie and the baby giggled and ran around, filling the house with cheerful chaos. Christy found herself laughing more than she had in weeks, and for brief moments, the fear that had haunted her seemed to vanish.

Gene called several times throughout the day, checking in, asking how she was feeling, and talking about the children. His voice was a constant source of comfort. Each time he spoke, Christy felt a little stronger, a little more certain that she could face whatever was coming.

Sunday morning arrived, and with it, a quiet resolve. Christy dressed carefully, made sure the children were ready, and walked with Ellan to church. Gene followed a few minutes later, holding the baby in one arm and Sammie's hand in the other. For the first time in a long time, Christy felt a sense of solidarity—not just with Gene, but with her whole family. She wasn't alone anymore.

During the service, Christy focused on the words of the pastor, letting them fill her with calm and reassurance. She whispered a quiet prayer, asking for strength, protection, and guidance. The familiar rhythm of faith—the songs, the quiet moments of reflection—helped her center herself. She realized that while she couldn't control the voices, she could control her response to them.

After the service, while walking to the car, Ellan squeezed Christy's hand. "You're strong, honey. Remember that. You've made it this far, and we'll be right here for you every step of the way."

Christy nodded, feeling the warmth of her mother's words settle over her like a protective blanket. Gene smiled at her from the car, and she felt the courage she'd need for the coming week. The appointment with the doctor no longer seemed like a terrifying ordeal—it was the first step toward understanding, toward taking control.

As they drove home, Christy allowed herself a small smile. The voices hadn't come back yet, and maybe—just maybe—she could face them with help. Whatever lay ahead, she wouldn't face it alone. And for the first time in years, that made the world feel a little less frightening.

It was Wednesday morning, and Christy's appointment was scheduled for eleven o'clock. Gene had taken the day off to drive her to Pittsburgh to see the doctor. The physician Christy was going to see was reputed to be the best in the country, and Gene thought that if the doctor was as good as everyone said, maybe they would finally get some answers.

When they arrived at the office, Christy had to fill out the usual forms, and then they waited for her turn. Christy was extremely nervous—she paced the floor, unable to sit still. Gene told her to try to relax, but it did little good. She still feared the doctor would think she was crazy. She didn't tell Gene this, but she didn't have to; he seemed to know exactly what she was thinking.

Gene stood up, took her hand gently, and said, "Honey, try to relax. Everything will be okay. All you have to do is put your faith in God, and He will look after you." He smiled and squeezed her hand gently. Somehow, it helped. Christy felt a little of her tension ease. She knew that God was on her side, and that she had many people who loved her and were rooting for her. She resolved in her heart that she couldn't let them down.

The nurse came into the waiting room and asked Christy to come into the doctor's office. Gene stood to go in with her, but the nurse instructed him to stay in the waiting room until Christy had changed. Gene felt a bit upset, worried that he might not hear what the doctor said.

A few minutes later, the nurse returned to get Gene. "You thought I wasn't coming back?" she said with a smile. "Well, I fooled you, didn't I?" She explained how Gene could find the room where Christy was waiting and reassured him not to worry.

Gene followed her directions, his heart pounding with concern and anticipation.

Christy said, "If the doctor doesn't know how to treat me, he'll send me to someone who does."

Gene found the room where Christy was waiting and opened the door. Christy looked up and saw him—she was happy. She had thought maybe they wouldn't let him in while the doctor examined her.

Gene went straight to her, kissed her, and said, "You looked surprised. You didn't think I'd let you go through this alone, did you?"

Christy smiled and said, "No. I knew I could count on you."

The doctor entered the room, and Christy immediately tensed. He was not what she had expected—she had anticipated an older man, but instead, he was a very handsome, middle-aged man. Even Gene had expected someone older, but neither of them cared as long as the doctor could help Christy.

The doctor introduced himself and asked Christy to explain what had been happening to her. She did, and then he asked, "How long has this been going on?"

Christy replied, "As long as I can remember."

The doctor inquired further, "About how old were you when it started?"

Christy said, "That's easy."

"How's that?" the doctor asked.

"The first time was when I was found down by the creek, half-drowned," Christy explained.

The doctor said, "Can you tell me exactly what happened that day?"

Christy nodded. "Yes, I'll try." She began to recount the picnic. "We were at a picnic of some kind. There were a lot of children around. We were playing games and having a very good time." She grew quiet and dropped her head, almost afraid to continue.

"Go on, Christy. Tell me about it," the doctor encouraged gently. "Nothing will hurt you now. That was a long time ago."

Christy hesitated. The doctor said softly, "Help me help you, honey. Talk to me."

She looked at Gene. He nodded, giving her the courage to continue. She recounted the events of that day in detail.

After she finished, the doctor asked, "So the voices were the reason you ended up down at the creek, right?"

"Yes, that's right," Christy confirmed.

"Tell me more about the voices," the doctor pressed. "Do they remind you of someone you know?"

Christy shook her head. "No, not really."

"Then why are you so compelled to follow them?"

"I'm not really sure," Christy admitted. "The longer they call my name, the more I am led by them… almost like they put me in a trance or something."

The doctor asked, "What do they sound like?"

"They sound very far away at first and very sad," Christy explained. "If I try to ignore them, they come closer and get demanding. After that, I don't remember much, only that when I come back to reality, I find myself in dangerous situations."

"Can you explain?" the doctor asked. "So I know what situations you mean."

"Like down at the creek that day," Christy said. "I thought I died."

The doctor looked puzzled and asked her to continue. Christy said, "The voices called me to the water. When I was standing at the edge, it felt like something pushed me in. The water wasn't very deep, so I thought I could get out. I tried, but I couldn't get my head above the water. Something was holding me down."

She stopped, hanging her head, and cried. The doctor gave her something to calm her. After a while, she began to speak again.

The doctor asked, "How do you feel now?"

"I'm okay," Christy said.

"Christy, can you tell me why you didn't die that day?" the doctor asked.

"If I tell you, you won't believe me," she replied.

"Christy, I'm here to help you, and I will believe anything you tell me. I don't think you came all this way to lie. Please go on."

Christy nodded. "Okay. When I was under the water, I was fighting to get free. Something was holding my head down. I thought my hair must be caught in debris, so I reached my hand over my head to free it. But it wasn't caught, and still, I couldn't lift my head. Something was holding me down. I struggled, but it was no use. My lungs hurt so badly. I needed to breathe. I opened my mouth, and water gushed in. Then I felt something grab me under my arms. All I remember after that is waking up on the creek bank, dripping wet and covered in mud."

She looked around, but there was no one there.

The doctor asked if that was the only time something like this had happened.

"Oh no," Christy said. "I've had more experiences." She went on to recount all the other lives she had seen.

By this time, two hours had passed in Christy's session. The doctor asked if, the next time she came in, she would be willing to go into another life for him.

Christy replied, "I'll try."

"Fine," the doctor said. "Now I'm going to give you a prescription. Take it three times a day. It's very important that you follow this exactly."

Christy nodded. "I'll do anything that will help."

The doctor turned to Gene. "Is there a way someone could be with Christy while she's taking the pills?"

"Yes," Gene said. "We'll work something out."

Christy spoke up again. "What will the medicine do?"

"It will relax you," the doctor explained.

Christy shook her head. "No. I won't take it. When I relax, that's when the voices come."

The doctor reassured her, "This medicine will relax your mind as well as your body. It will help you sleep without dreaming or hearing the voices. But if it doesn't work, I want you to call me immediately. Agreed?"

Christy nodded. "Yes."

With that, she and Gene went through the door to schedule her next appointment, and then they headed home.

As soon as the couple left, the doctor returned to rewind the recording of Christy's session. He listened to it carefully, rewound it again, and played it a third time. Concern etched his face.

He called out to his nurse. "Get in touch with Dr. Whitman and have him on the line immediately."

Even as he saw his next patient, Christy remained on his mind. He worried that she might be drawn toward self-destruction. He hoped the medicine would help, at least until they had some answers.

After finishing with his patient, Dr. Whitman called back. The two doctors discussed Christy's case and agreed to be present together at her next session. Dr. Whitman promised to research the field before her next visit.

Dr. Shaw thanked him and said he would keep in touch. "I'm extremely worried about Christy," he added.

Dr. Whitman replied gravely, "And with good reason. I had a patient once who heard voices… she committed suicide."

Dr. Shaw's face paled. "Dear God… I have to help this girl somehow. I just can't let that happen to her."

"I understand," Dr. Whitman said. "We'll do what we can. Let me know when her next appointment is, and I'll be there."

The doctors hung up. Dr. Shaw called the nurse again to check Christy's next appointment.

"In two weeks," the nurse said.

"No," Dr. Shaw said firmly. "I want to see her next week."

The nurse explained that there were no openings.

"Make an opening! Dammit! I need to see this girl!" Dr. Shaw demanded.

The nurse juggled the schedule and managed to book Christy for the first appointment of the week.

Gene and Christy didn't get out much alone, so they decided to stop and have dinner on their way home.

When they arrived at the restaurant, Christy called Ellan to check on the children and let her mom know they would be home soon. Ellan reassured her, "Take your time. Everything's fine here."

"Great," Christy said. "We're going to get something to eat and then head home." She hung up and returned to meet Gene at their table, where he had already ordered coffee for them.

Christy sat down and glanced over the menu. After deciding what to eat, they continued their conversation while waiting for the waitress. When the waitress arrived to take their order, they picked up right where they left off, enjoying each other's company. They spent the next couple of hours at the table, simply making up for lost time.

At one point, Christy asked, "What did you think of the doctor?"

Gene replied, "I liked him. But if he can't give us some answers, we'll find someone who can."

They didn't have to worry about Dr. Shaw—ever since their session, he had been thinking of nothing else but Christy's case.

When Gene and Christy returned to her mother's house, there was a message waiting. Ellan told her that the doctor's office had called to reschedule her appointment. She now had to be at the office next Monday at ten o'clock.

Christy looked at Gene with a worried expression, then back at her mom. "Are you sure, Mom?"

"Yes, absolutely," Ellan said. "I spoke to the nurse myself. That's what she said."

Christy turned back to Gene in a strange, bewildered tone. "See? I told you—they think I'm crazy. I'm not going back. I don't care what happens, I'm not going back."

Gene and Ellan tried to reason with her, but it did no good. In Christy's mind, the doctor wanted to prove she was crazy and commit her. The subject was dropped.

Ellan and Gene decided to wait a couple of days before talking to her about it again. Right now, it was pointless.

By the end of the week, Christy had mellowed enough to agree to go back to the doctor. The medicine she was taking had helped. The week went quickly for Christy; she floated through it. She said she felt like she was on cloud nine. The pills relaxed her completely—her speech was slower, and her reactions weren't as quick as normal. That was likely the reason the doctor wanted someone with her at all times, especially around the children.

If something happened to one of the children, Christy wouldn't be able to respond quickly enough to help them. This was a very good reason for Christy and Gene to stay with Ellan and Jake; that way, Christy would never be alone. Gene was thankful for this arrangement because he had to work through the weekend, yet he wanted to be with her when she saw the doctor on Monday. Besides, he couldn't afford to just take off. Christy hadn't returned to work since the baby was born.

The week passed, and now it was Sunday evening. All day, they had kept themselves busy. They started the morning by going to church and then took a long drive into the country to visit relatives. Jake and Ellan came along, and everyone had a good time.

On the way home, they stopped at Christy's aunt's house. It was almost dinner time, and her aunt insisted they eat with the family. After the meal and the dishes were done, everyone retired to the front porch to sit and chat. The conversation naturally turned to Christy's appointment with the doctor the next morning. Christy's aunt was shocked.

"I had no idea anything was wrong," she said. "Why didn't someone tell me?"

Ellan explained gently, "I thought it was Christy's place to tell whoever she wanted, and I didn't take the liberty to discuss it with anyone."

Late that evening, they all decided it was time to head home. Christy was very tired, and Gene helped her get the children ready for bed. While they worked together bathing the kids, the subject of the doctor came up again. The more they talked about it, the more reluctant Christy became. She didn't want to see the doctor.

"Honey, why are you fighting this?" Gene asked.

Christy screamed, "That's a stupid question!" She was angry with him. Gene knew exactly why—she feared the doctor would commit her to an asylum.

Gene dropped the towels on the floor and went to Christy, wrapping his arms around her and holding her close. "Honey, you worry too much. Everything will work out. Trust me, okay? I promise I won't let anything happen to you. I'll take care of you. You mean the world to me, and I can't live without you. I couldn't bear the thought of living without you by my side."

Christy relaxed slightly in his arms, feeling the comfort and protection only Gene could provide.

Christy seemed to be feeling a little better after their talk. They decided to get ready for bed because they had to start early in the morning. But even going to bed didn't help Christy. She didn't sleep a wink all night. Fear kept her tossing and turning; over and over, she thought the doctor was going to give her bad news. The night seemed endless.

Finally, the sun came up, and it was time to get ready. Around seven, Gene got out of bed and showered. He went to the kitchen to make coffee. Christy knew she had to get ready but couldn't pull herself out of bed. She lay there for over an hour, staring at the ceiling.

After finishing half a pot of coffee, Gene came to check on her. He went back to the bedroom and opened the door. Christy was sitting on the edge of the bed.

"Honey, you'll have to get a move on, or we'll be late," Gene said gently.

Christy screamed at him. "Don't you dare tell me what to do! And don't rush me, or I won't go at all!"

Gene just looked at her. He knew exactly how she felt and thought he'd probably feel the same way in her shoes. Softly, he said, "Come on, honey, please? We have to do this for us."

With a little coaxing, Christy finally got ready, with Gene helping her along. They were lucky the traffic wasn't too bad and arrived at the doctor's office on time.

When Christy was called in, she hesitated at the door. Inside, she saw another man. She knew he was a doctor and immediately got scared. She pulled back, and Gene caught her by the arm. All Christy could think was that she wanted to go home.

Dr. Shaw approached her and said, "Christy, this is Dr. Whitman. He's here because I asked him to be. He is a doctor like myself, though in a different field. He has experience with patients who have had past-life experiences, some similar to what you are experiencing. He may be able to help us get some answers. I would like him to stay and listen. Is that okay with you?"

Christy looked at her husband and remembered his words that morning. She heard the reassurance in her head and trusted him. She told Dr. Shaw, "Yes, that's okay."

Dr. Shaw helped Christy get comfortable on the sofa. He asked her simple questions, like, "How are you today?" Christy answered, and they carried on the conversation for a short time. The doctor tried to help her relax as much as possible.

Finally, he said, "Christy, I want you to listen to my voice and relax. Just hear my voice and shut everything else out. Concentrate on my voice. You're feeling tired now, and you want to sleep. Just relax and let the sound of my voice enter your mind. Now, you're asleep. Can you hear me, Christy?"

Christy was totally relaxed. Her mind was open, but she was asleep. She could hear the doctor and answer his questions. She was now hypnotized.

Dr. Shaw began by asking her questions about her childhood. He wanted to find out if something traumatic had happened that could explain her problem. After several questions, he concluded that Christy had a good childhood and that her issue originated from another source.

Dr. Shaw was ready to complete the session when he asked Christy if she would answer some questions for Dr. Whitman. She said, "If you wish."

Dr. Shaw said, "Yes, that's what I wish. Is that okay?"

Christy nodded. Dr. Whitman sat down and began to ask her questions. She felt comfortable with him, so he continued. He asked nearly all the same questions that Dr. Shaw had, only worded differently. It didn't matter; Christy answered them all the same.

Soon, Dr. Whitman asked her if she could go into another life. Christy said, "I'll try."

The doctor instructed, "When you go to another life, I need to know everything that happens, okay?"

"Yes, I will," Christy replied.

Dr. Whitman took his time and guided Christy into another life. The look on her face told him when she had entered the other time.

"Christy, where are you right now?" he asked.

"I really don't know," she said. "I'm in a town… a big town."

The doctor asked, "What kind of streets are there?"

Christy hesitated. "Not sure… can't see clearly. Oh yes, now I can see them—they're made of stone. The buildings are made of stone too. They're very old. Horses are pulling wagons and carriages in the streets. People are all around, selling their wares on the street and in small huts."

Dr. Whitman nodded. "Okay, Christy, that's good. Now, who are you?"

Christy whispered, "Don't know."

"Can you find out?" the doctor asked.

"Yes… I need to see myself somehow."

She glanced down the street at a watering trough. "Maybe my reflection will tell me… almost there."

Christy was quiet for some time. The doctor asked her questions, but she didn't answer. He had to speak more firmly before she finally responded.

"Christy, is something wrong?" he asked.

"Yes… very wrong," she replied.

"Tell me what's wrong," he pressed.

"Ugly… very ugly," Christy said.

"What's ugly?" the doctor asked.

"Face in the water… can't be me. Face ugly… all scarred, like burns or something," she said.

The doctor said, "I want you to go back into this life. Tell me what you know about the scars. Can you do that?"

"I'll try," Christy whispered. She sat quietly for a moment and then began to describe the other life.

Walking down the street, people laugh at me, and babies cry when I get close to them. People are cruel. They throw things at me and hit me. They call me names. They say I'm ugly.

I try to cover my face so they can't see me, but it does no good—they still laugh and strike me. They throw rocks. They hurt me. The clothes I wear are all rags, and I'm hungry. I can't find any food to steal, and when I beg, they only laugh and call me names. I feel like I'm starving to death.

It's almost dark. I have to hurry home to the stable where I sleep. I'm afraid of the dark—bad things happen in the dark. People hurt me. I have to hurry. I run and run, almost there, just around the corner.

I look around the corner, and the alley is dark. I hear voices. I'm so scared. The voices are getting nearer, and I can't get around them. I must go on—it's the only way home.

There, in the shadows, I can see them. Men and women, all laughing. They have a jug of ale and are coming after me. Something hits me—it hurts. Again, I'm struck. They're beating and kicking me. Oh God! The pain—I can't stand it. Why are they doing this to me?

I try to run, but I fall. My leg must be broken—I can't stand up. I try to crawl, but they're still beating me, laughing at me. I can't get away. Something hits me on the head, and everything goes dark.

I try to see, but I can't. My eyes… I've gone blind. Finally, the beating stops, and they all run away. I'm lying in the middle of the street, I think. All I hear are the sounds of horses' hooves on the street. They seem to be getting closer and closer.

It sounds like lots of horses, running fast. I have to get out of the way. I can't get up—my body, my legs won't work. The pain is so bad I can't stand to move. But I have to. The horses are almost here. I crawl, in terrible pain.

Merciful Jesus! They're here. I feel the weight of them on my body, crushing me, rolling me down the street under their hooves. I'm all twisted up in their legs, and the pain is intense.

Then, suddenly, I can't feel anything. I'm numb. I'm fading fast. I'm dying.

Gene looked across the room. He couldn't believe his eyes and ears. The look of horror on Christy's face made him shiver. She was trembling, tears running down her cheeks, curled up in a ball. Gene's eyes filled with tears. His heart ached for his wife, and he felt so helpless.

The doctors stood over her, watching her reactions and making sure she wasn't in any danger. After a short time, Christy lay still in a ball. One had to really strain to see her breathing, and then the doctor decided it was best to bring her out of hypnosis. She was now too close to danger.

Dr. Whitman called to Christy. "Christy, can you hear me? Wherever you are, you must come back."

Christy didn't respond. The doctor called again. "Christy, can you hear me? Try, Christy, try."

Still nothing.

The doctor's tone grew more commanding. "Christy, come back. There's nothing to be afraid of. Come back to our present time. There's no danger here. You'll be alright, I promise. Now please—open your eyes and come back to us."

Slowly, Christy opened her eyes and drew in a deep breath of air. She was still trembling, but she was awake. The doctor touched her arm. "Are you okay?"

Christy said, "Yes… I think so."

But just then, panic flashed across her face. She threw her head from side to side, looking for something. The doctor asked, "What is it, Christy? What's wrong?"

She asked, "The horses… where are the horses?"

Then she realized the horses were in another time, another life.

Christy sat up on the sofa, staring at the floor for a long time. When she finally spoke, it was to ask the doctor if he thought she was crazy.

Dr. Whitman took her hand and said firmly, "Absolutely not. Christy, we're going to help you. It will take time, but I think we can find the answers you've been looking for. All we need from you is patience, okay?"

Christy said, "I'll try, but it's hard to be patient when someone—or something—is nagging you over and over."

The doctor nodded. "Yes, Christy, I understand. It won't be easy, but if you continue taking the medicine we gave you, it'll help. So don't forget to take your pills, okay?"

He turned to Gene. "Gene, you can take your girl home now. I want to see her next week at the same time."

Gene said, "I'll be sure she gets there."

The doctors shook Gene's hand, said goodbye to Christy, and watched them leave. After Gene and Christy had gone, the doctors discussed the case. They agreed they would need to work together—it was a very difficult case. Two heads were better than one, and they knew that without their help, Christy could be lost.

CHAPTER
Six

Another Place, Another Life

Christy and Gene were about halfway home. They were discussing the doctors and Christy's session. Christy told Gene that she liked the doctors and felt very comfortable with them. Gene took his eyes off the road long enough to look at Christy and smiled. "I'm glad, honey," he said, "and I liked them too."

But all the while he was talking to Christy, he couldn't stop thinking about the session and how helpless he had felt when she was under hypnosis. He remembered watching Christy as she writhed and twisted, shouting, *"They're beating me!"* She looked as though she were the one being beaten and tormented. She screamed continuously and rolled around on the sofa as the session went on. Finally, at the very end, she bolted upright into a sitting position and collapsed. Gene thought that, at that moment, the person whose life she was living must have died.

Even while driving, Gene couldn't shake the thought of all the torment his wife had been going through. His heart ached for the one he loved. He realized he couldn't do anything to help her, and that made him feel even worse. At this point, he had to be very careful with what he said to Christy—she had been extremely sensitive lately. He worried that she might think he didn't love her anymore and only stayed with her out of pity, which was far from the truth.

He sincerely loved Christy. Now that he had seen with his own eyes what was happening, he understood how hard it had been for her and that she had been dealing with something beyond her control. He thought that it was time to get her problem taken care of. She had been tormented all her life, and it was time to put it all to rest.

The remaining half of the trip home from the doctors was a quiet ride. Christy was lost in thought about the session, and Gene was thinking about the fear Christy had been living in.

They finally pulled into the driveway at Jake and Ellan's house. When they went inside, they found that the children were napping. Jake immediately wanted to know how things went at the doctors.

Christy said, "Everything went just fine. I'm tired—can I go lie down for a while, and then I'll tell you everything?"

Jake nodded. "Sure, we don't mind."

Christy went upstairs to rest with the children. While she was napping, Gene spoke with Jake and Ellan, explaining everything that had happened at the doctors. When he finished, Jake sat with his head in his hands, and Ellan was weeping.

Ellan looked at Gene with tears in her eyes. "My poor baby... the hell and torment she must be going through."

Jake raised his head long enough to say, "If there is anything we can do, we'll do it. No matter what it is. Understood?"

Gene replied, "Yes, I understand. And thank you so much for everything you've already done." He added that Christy loved and respected them both very much, and that it was very important to her that they knew it.

The following week went along smoothly. Christy was feeling much better, and the medicine was really helping. It had been almost three weeks since she had heard the voices, and even longer since she had a past life experience. Everyone was pleased and prayed that it might all be over.

But little did they know, it was like the calm before the storm. They all agreed to live one day at a time, which made things easier to manage.

The week flew by. Monday morning arrived, and Gene did the same thing as the week before—he had worked through the weekend so he could be with Christy. He was very interested in what would happen during her next hypnosis session.

This time, Dr. Whitman wanted to talk to Christy about the voices. She told him about them. After hearing enough, he explained that he wanted to hypnotize her again. Since she hadn't heard the voices for a couple of weeks, he hoped Christy could try to contact them.

At first, Christy refused. She told the doctor the voices were evil and wanted to hurt her. The doctor reassured her that she had nothing to fear, and that if she appeared to be in any danger, he would bring her back immediately. Only then did she agree.

The doctor proceeded. It wasn't long before Christy was fully hypnotized. Gene just sat quietly and watched. He, as well as the doctors, didn't know what to expect.

The doctor encouraged Christy to call out for the voices. She tried, but there was no response. So the doctor asked the next best question: how had the voices contacted her the first time?

Christy replied, "I don't know. They started talking to me when I was just old enough to remember. They only call me when they want to—and they're not ready now. They'll come when they want to."

The doctor asked, "Christy, are they talking to you now?"

"Yes," she whispered, "and they're very angry. Please don't let them hurt me."

Tears streamed down her face.

The doctor asked, "Do they want to hurt you?"

"Yes. They're evil," Christy said.

"How do you know they're evil?" he asked.

"I can feel it. They want to destroy me," she replied.

The doctor said firmly, "Okay, Christy. I want you to wake up now."

But Christy didn't wake. Gene grew anxious. He saw her trembling and sobbing, and he feared the doctor wouldn't be able to bring her back. He opened his mouth to speak, but the doctor shook his head—no words.

The doctor's voice grew louder and more commanding. "Christy, wake up—right now!"

Her eyes flew open instantly. She wiped the tears from her cheeks and looked at the doctors, then at Gene.

"What happened?" she asked, confused. She didn't remember anything that had just occurred.

The doctor explained, "The voices contacted you, and they were upset."

Christy's face filled with terror. The doctor reassured her, "Don't worry. As long as you take your medicine, you'll be fine."

Dr. Whitman then turned to Dr. Shaw. "Would the same time next Monday work for Christy's next appointment?"

Dr. Shaw replied, "Yes—if it's okay with Christy and Gene."

It was.

After Christy and Gene left to head home, the doctors discussed the session. Dr. Whitman told Dr. Shaw that he had never seen anything like this in all his years of practice. He said that the experiences Christy was having were definitely past lives, but the voices didn't fit in.

Dr. Shaw asked, "Do you think she's right? Do they want to destroy her?"

Dr. Whitman replied, "I really don't know. But one thing is for sure—we had better find out before it's too late, in case she is right. We'll just have to keep working with her and pray that we find the answers we need. And we need to do this as soon as possible."

By the tone of Dr. Whitman's voice, Dr. Shaw knew he was very worried about Christy. Dr. Whitman told Dr. Shaw that he had to get going—he had other patients and a lot of research to do. The two doctors bid each other good day.

Christy continued her weekly visits to the doctors for the next two months. The therapy was helping her. She felt like a completely different person. She slept well and relaxed when she needed to, without assistance.

However, those who cared for her still weren't sure how she truly felt. Someone was always checking in on her.

One day, her mother was out shopping and stopped by to see how Christy was doing. She asked if Christy needed anything.

Christy answered harshly, almost screaming, "No! I don't need anything! I'm sick and tired of everyone treating me like I'm incompetent. I can take care of myself!"

She shouted at Ellan and cursed. Ellan was very upset. This was not like Christy at all. Christy had never raised her voice to her mother, no matter how much they disagreed. Ellan realized she had to act to calm Christy down. She didn't dare ask if Christy had taken her medicine, so she just tried to talk to her—but it was no use.

Ellan became frightened. She had never seen Christy like this and didn't know what to do. Finally, she thought of the only thing she could do: she told Christy that she was going to take the children for a walk.

Ellan went straight to Marion's house and explained what had happened. Marion said, "We'd better call and try to get hold of Gene—and call the doctor."

The two women made the calls as quickly as they could, then waited anxiously for responses. They felt helpless.

At Christy's house, she was running around, talking to someone—or rather, to something. She was in a trance of some kind. She yelled, "Leave me alone! Just go away! I'm not listening to you! You're going to hurt me!"

Then she went silent. The battle had been won. The voices had taken over. Christy moved in a zombie-like state. She went to the wall where the car keys hung, took them down, and headed for the car.

Ellan saw her and tried to stop her, but Christy pushed her aside. Ellan fell to the ground. By the time she got back on her feet, Christy had already pulled away. Ellan screamed for Marion, who ran immediately to meet her at the door.

Ellan explained what had just happened. Marion grabbed the phone and called the job where Gene worked. She told his boss to have Gene come home immediately—it was urgent. The message was delivered, and Gene called Marion right away.

"Christy's in a bad way," Marion said. "She's in the car and headed for the interstate."

Gene thought for a moment. "Which way is she going?" he asked. Then he gave instructions: "Call Jake. Tell him to head south. I'll go north. Maybe we can intercept her before anything happens." He hung up and raced for the highway.

Marion called Jake and relayed the message. "I'm on my way," he said. "Take care of Ellan for me."

"Don't worry, I will," Marion replied.

Jake prayed silently as he drove away. *Please, God, look after my little girl.* Then he headed south.

Christy was headed north. She drove at a dangerously high speed, with no idea where she was going. She was simply following the voices. They commanded her to accelerate, and she obeyed.

Her face was blank, her eyes staring straight ahead but seeing nothing. She was no longer driving—*the voices were driving the car.*

Christy was just sitting behind the wheel, her mind blank except for the voices. *"Faster... drive faster,"* they urged. And she obeyed. The speedometer climbed—ninety-five miles per hour and rising. She passed every vehicle on the road without even noticing. She felt nothing—no fear, no pain. Only the voices existed.

Then, all of a sudden, Christy snapped out of it. She looked ahead and froze. A woman was standing in the middle of the highway. Christy slammed on the brakes. At the speed she was traveling, the car skidded sideways. She fought for control, but the vehicle spun out of her grasp. It whirled several times before coming to rest on its side against the median bank.

Christy, almost in shock, looked through the windshield and couldn't believe her eyes. A small airplane had belly-flopped onto the road just in front of her. It skidded across all four lanes before crashing nose-first into the hillside. The impact triggered an explosion. Flames engulfed the plane as debris flew everywhere. Part of the tail section slammed onto the trunk of Christy's car, shattering the rear window. Glass littered the seats and floor.

She sat frozen, gripping the steering wheel as though her hands were molded to it. People began to gather around the crash site, some approaching Christy's car. They tried to speak to her, but she didn't respond. A young couple quickly fetched blankets from their car and stayed with her until emergency vehicles arrived.

Paramedics reached Christy first. They checked her vitals as she slowly came to.

"What… what happened? Where am I?" she asked, her voice trembling.

"You'll be okay, ma'am," one paramedic said, reaching into his kit. As he moved to one side, Christy could see over him. Her eyes fell on the plane on the other side of the road, and the memory of the crash flooded back.

A man's voice cut through the chaos. *"Are you crazy? You damn fool! You could have killed someone pulling a stunt like that!"* The paramedic, focused on Christy, had no idea why this man was shouting. He didn't yet know that Christy had no connection to the plane crash—or that she may have inadvertently caused the chain of accidents on the highway.

After a short while, Gene arrived at the crash site. He caught a glimpse of Christy's car ahead but couldn't drive close because of the chaos. He pulled off the road and ran toward her. As he moved down the highway, he couldn't believe the scene before him—cars and trucks piled up everywhere, people injured and bleeding. A sick feeling settled in the pit of his stomach. Deep down, he feared that Christy had caused it all.

He was terrified to see her, worried she might be badly hurt—or worse. But he had to reach her as quickly as possible. When he finally arrived at Christy's car, she was still sitting in the front seat. Relief washed over him. *Thank you, Jesus,* he whispered.

He ran to her, ready to speak, but a paramedic intercepted him. "Who are you?" the man asked.

"I'm her husband," Gene said, breathless.

The paramedic explained that they were sending Christy to the hospital for precautionary checks. They carefully helped her into an ambulance, and she was on her way to the nearest hospital. Gene followed as closely as he could, navigating the tangled mess of wreckage by moving along the shoulder and median until he cleared the congestion.

When he finally arrived at the hospital, Christy was already in with the doctor. Gene was surprised at how quickly they had gotten her inside. The waiting room was crowded with people from the accident. He found the room where Christy was being attended and arrived just in time to hear the doctor say they were going to admit her.

Gene felt a surge of panic—he had feared the worst—but the doctor reassured him. "Just overnight," he said. "We want to make sure there's no fracture to the skull. She hit her head pretty hard." Relief flooded Gene.

While Christy was being prepared for her room, Gene made a few urgent phone calls. He called Jake and Ellan first. Jake had just returned home when he heard about the accident on the north side of the highway. He immediately feared Christy had been involved, and relief flooded him when he learned she was okay. He'd heard on the radio that there had been fatalities in the crash.

After hanging up, Jake asked Marion to watch the children so he and Ellan could head to the hospital. Marion agreed immediately. They quickly gathered themselves and rushed out the door, determined to get to Christy as soon as possible.

Marion was fixing the children something to eat when the phone rang. It was Dr. Shaw returning her call. Marion explained what had happened, and Dr. Shaw immediately contacted Dr. Whitman. Both doctors headed to the hospital to see Christy. They needed to understand what had really happened and why she had been in such a state before the accident.

When they arrived at the hospital, Gene was still in the room with Christy. Ellan and Jake had gone to the coffee shop to get something to drink. Christy noticed the doctors and asked Gene, "What are they doing here?"

Dr. Shaw said, "We're just here to talk to you. We need to understand what happened today."

Christy snapped in a harsh tone, "Nothing happened today! What are you talking about?"

Just then, Ellan entered the room. She asked, "Christy, do you remember me being at the house with you?"

Christy shook her head. "No, Mom, I don't. Why?"

Ellan gently explained what had occurred earlier that afternoon. Christy looked dumbfounded. She had no idea she had treated her mother so poorly. "Oh, Mom, I'm so sorry! I had no idea," she said, her voice trembling.

Ellan went to her, tears in her eyes, and hugged her tightly. As they embraced, both of them cried. Gene and Jake watched, their own eyes growing watery.

Finally, Ellan told Christy that she should talk to the doctors. Christy nodded and agreed, realizing it was time to explain everything.

Dr. Whitman spoke gently to Christy. "I want you to tell me everything you can remember."

Christy began, her voice trembling. "I was working around the house, playing with the kids… I remember being in the kitchen…" She trailed off, going silent.

Dr. Whitman asked softly, "Christy, what's wrong?"

After a few moments, she said, "That's all I can remember… until I found myself on the highway."

"Okay, Christy," the doctor said calmly. "I'm going to hypnotize you. Relax, and listen only to the sound of my voice. Breathe deeply… just relax."

Christy's body softened as she went under hypnosis. Dr. Whitman began asking questions about her day, starting from when she got out of bed. She responded clearly, answering all his initial questions.

Then he asked, "Did anyone visit you today?"

At that, Christy's face contorted with horror. She began shaking and rolling back and forth on the bed. Ellan watched in disbelief as Christy started mumbling, as if arguing with someone. Her voice grew louder: "Leave me alone! I'm not going with you! Just go away!"

She screamed at whoever she imagined was there. Tears streamed down her face as she thrashed in the bed, trembling uncontrollably.

Dr. Whitman spoke firmly. "Christy, I need you to talk to me. If you can't answer, on the count of three, I want you to wake up. One… two… three… Christy, are you awake?"

She didn't respond.

Raising his voice now, the doctor commanded, "Christy, wake up!"

This time, she opened her eyes. Seeing Dr. Whitman bent over her, she bolted upright, throwing her arms around his neck. "Please… help me!" she pleaded. "They wouldn't let me go! They said they needed me… they tried to take me with them!"

Dr. Whitman gently reassured her. "Christy, you never left the hospital. You're still here, safe in bed."

Christy looked around and saw Gene and her mother and father in the room.

"That's right, honey," Gene said softly. "You're right here with us."

Christy slumped back into the bed, exhausted. "But it felt so real," she whispered.

"In your mind, Christy," Dr. Whitman said, "it was real. But you are safe. You'll be okay. Between Dr. Shaw and me, we're going to help you."

He continued, "We're going to double your medicine. You'll need someone with you at all times. I want to see you twice a week. And no driving, understood?"

"Yes, I promise," Christy replied.

The doctors left the room, and Gene followed them. He needed answers. Catching them just as they were about to get on the elevator, he rode down with them.

"I know you're busy," he said, "but I need to know what's happening to Christy."

Dr. Shaw asked kindly, "Do you want a cup of coffee while we talk?"

Sitting in the coffee shop, Dr. Whitman explained. "Christy is in great danger. She is right—the voices are trying to destroy her. We don't know why or how. We believe the voices drew her to the accident site today. Why she didn't die… we have no explanation. Something saved her—maybe a miracle, or whatever one believes. But clearly, she was meant to die."

He looked Gene in the eye. "We have to help her. It's critical that you stand by her. She needs you and her family more than ever right now."

Gene nodded firmly and returned to Christy, determination in his heart.

On his way down the hall to the elevator, Gene's mind was on Christy. He had been wondering how they would manage the house and the children. Christy couldn't be alone, and he had to work. All the bills from the doctors were starting to pile up, not to mention all the regular bills—car payments and insurance premiums.

Then he realized that they were very fortunate to have car insurance. With the accident, they were really going to need it.

Gene then thought about the accident. He really didn't know what happened, but he definitely thought the worst. He didn't know how much of it Christy was responsible for. And then he thought about all the unfortunate people who died in the crash. He shuddered to think that Christy may have been the cause of all those deaths.

Not to mention how Christy would handle the situation in her delicate condition. Gene thought of the impact it would have on her.

As Gene turned the corner to Christy's room, he stood outside the door and looked up and said a small but very sincere prayer.

"Dear Lord, we don't ask for much, and I sure hope you're listening."

Just then Gene broke down. He cried so hard his knees started to buckle under him. Jake came out of the room just in time to catch Gene before he hit the floor.

Jake said to Gene, "With all our faith, the Lord will see us through. I just know He will."

Jake and Gene stood in the hall until Gene got himself together. Jake hugged Gene and said, "We're all in this together, son, and we will make it through if we all stick together."

Jake patted Gene on the shoulder and said, "There's a very important lady waiting for you, young man. You had better hustle before she starts to throw things."

They both smiled and went into the room.

Ellan was getting a little tired, so she and Jake decided to go home. They told Christy and Gene not to worry about the little ones—they would take them home.

Christy then had a whole list of things for Ellan to do, like what clothes to put on the children and what to take to feed them.

Gene told her not to worry. Ellan was very well trained in that field, and the kids would be fine.

Christy smiled at her mother and said, "I'm sorry, Mom. I'm sure you can handle it. It's just that I've never been away from them before."

Ellan kissed her and said, "Rest and don't worry. I love you. I'll see you tomorrow."

Gene and Christy were alone. They decided to watch television awhile. Gene turned it on and the news was just coming on. He asked Christy if she wanted it turned, and she said no—that the news was fine.

The headline story was of the accident on the highway. Gene really didn't want Christy to hear about the accident because of all the people who died, but she insisted on seeing it.

When the newscaster showed pictures of the crash, Christy's car was the first car they aired. Christy stared at the television. She could hear nothing else. She was concentrating on what was being said.

When she heard how many people died, she slumped back in the bed.

Gene said to her, "Honey, are you okay?"

She didn't answer him. She just kept watching.

They showed pictures of the plane, then of the pileup of cars. It was a tangled mess. Tractor trailers were jackknifed and lying on top of cars, and smoke was everywhere. Cars were on fire and the plane had been burning. Emergency vehicles were everywhere too.

The crash site was too much for Christy to handle, but she wouldn't take her eyes off it.

She finally spoke after several minutes.

"My God. Look what I've done. I killed all those innocent people."

Then she went silent.

She had gone into a deep state of depression. She wouldn't talk at all to Gene. She just lay there and stared into space with a blank look on her face. Gene tried to get her to talk to him, but there was no use. She couldn't even hear him.

Gene got really nervous and ran down the hall to get a nurse.

The nurse came right away. She checked Christy and told Gene that she was going to give her a sedative that would calm her down and help her sleep.

Gene asked the nurse if he could stay awhile, and she told him only until she went to sleep. She really needed to sleep.

Gene said he would leave as soon as she fell asleep.

Then the nurse told Gene that they would call if they needed him and said good night.

Christy was sleeping calmly.

Gene tiptoed over to the bed. He bent over her and kissed her gently and whispered, "I love you, sweety. Please be okay. I need you, and the kids need you too."

A tear ran down his cheek as he turned and walked out of the room.

As he walked through the parking lot, he thought of Christy being in the hospital. The closer he got to the car, the more he felt like he was leaving something behind.

He tried to push the feeling aside and went home to see the children. At this point they needed at least one of their parents. For right now Gene was all they had until Christy got home.

With that thought in mind, he went straight home to his family.

He was real anxious to see the kids and thought of all kinds of questions they might ask him about their mom. He decided he would worry about that when the time came.

He pulled the car into the driveway and went into the house. The children were already in bed.

Gene felt a little relieved to find the kids in bed. He wanted to talk to Ellan and Jake anyway, and it would be a little difficult to keep a conversation going with the little ones around.

Gene went into the living room with Jake. The eleven o'clock news came on. Jake called Ellan in to watch the news.

The three of them sat with their ears glued to the television.

The top story was the accident on the highway, and they all sat thinking the same thing—was Christy the cause of all that mess and all those injuries?

But as they listened, they found out they were worried for nothing.

The police officer they interviewed first was saying that the accident was caused by the airplane crash.

They were all relieved to hear the news.

Gene jumped up in excitement and said, "I knew in my heart that Christy didn't cause all that mess and cause all those poor people to die."

Then he remembered that Christy was still thinking that she was the cause.

Gene started pacing the floor. His mind was racing.

"I have to let Christy know—but how?"

Ellan suggested that he call the hospital and talk to Christy's nurse, explain about the accident, and ask her to give the message to Christy.

Gene called the hospital and got hold of Christy's nurse. He explained about the accident and told the nurse how Christy felt responsible for all those deaths.

The nurse agreed that it would do a world of good for Christy to know that she was not at fault. The nurse promised Gene that she would deliver the message as soon as Christy woke up.

The nurse did as she had promised. As soon as Christy opened her eyes, the nurse gave her the news.

Christy looked at the nurse like she didn't believe her.

The nurse said, "It's true, honey. Call your husband. He'll tell you."

So Christy asked her what time it was. The nurse looked at her watch and told Christy that it was three in the morning.

Christy said, "Wow, it's really late."

But she knew that she had to talk to Gene.

She dialed the number and Jake answered the phone. Jake was worried that something was wrong.

"Are you okay?" he asked.

She said, "Yes, but I really need to talk to Gene. I got the message that Gene gave to the nurse. Dad, is it true?"

Jake said, "Yes, honey, it's true. You weren't the cause of all that mess."

The phone went silent.

Jake said, "Christy, are you okay?"

She said, "Yes. I was thanking the good Lord for looking after me."

Jake told Christy to hang on and said he would call Gene.

"I know he wants to talk to you too."

Gene got out of bed and walked down the hall to answer the phone. He was happy that Christy called him. He missed her very much.

He said, "Hi."

Christy said, "Honey, is it true? I know it must be, but I really need to hear it from you."

Gene said, "Yes, it's true, and everything is going to be alright. All we have to do is get you home where you belong, and everything will be fine."

Gene and Christy just talked awhile after that. He told her how much he loved and missed her.

Christy was crying on the phone.

Gene asked if something was wrong.

She said that she was just happy about the news.

Gene told her not to worry. Everything was going to be back to normal real soon.

Gene and Christy gave each other their love and said good night. They hung up the phones and went back to bed.

CHAPTER
Seven

Finding Lizzy

Christy couldn't go back to sleep. As she lay there, her mind raced. She was thinking about the day before—the accident, the voices, her mother, and all the other things that took place that day.

She couldn't rest. All those things kept going around in her head. She was exhausted, but her mind wouldn't stop. She thought she had to get some sleep, but sleep never came.

She called the nurse to see if she could get something to help her sleep. The nurse gave her some sleeping pills. She said that they would help her relax.

And that they did.

Christy relaxed, but sleep never came. Christy just lay there and relaxed. After a while, she simply started to slip away—away to another place and another time.

Christy now is standing in an open field. She's barely tall enough to see over the wheat she's standing in. She has no idea where she might be.

She hears voices off in the distance.

She follows the sound of the voices. They lead her to people working in cotton fields not far from where she found herself standing.

When she got to the people, a woman turned and said, "Child, where have you been? I've been worried sick to death about you."

The little girl didn't know where she had been and just said she was out walking.

The black lady was picking cotton. They had to hurry. The sun was going down and they were running out of time.

The little girl picked some cotton, but not much. Picking cotton hurts and makes your hands bleed, she said. And all the old people complained about their backs hurting from all the bending. Some could hardly stand the pain, but they still had to pick the cotton.

The sun had almost gone down when a man came riding up on a horse. Every worker in the field gathered their tools and headed in the direction of the man.

The black lady must be the little girl's mother because she was practically dragging the little girl to catch up with the other people.

The lady bent over and said to the little girl, "Child, you had best hurry or you might find yourself walking to the big house. Now come along and hurry."

The woman looked down the road and saw a wagon coming.

The lady said, "Hurry now."

They ran to catch the wagon.

The little girl was sure glad they caught it. The big house was quite a ways from the field.

When they got to the big house, the little girl just stopped and looked around. She was fascinated at what she saw.

The mother grabbed the little girl and said, "Child, what's got into you? You act like you never seen this place before. Now move along—we gots to git home."

Ahead of the girl was a place where the field hands lived. There were two rows of shacks, and they were all in need of repairs. But they were all livable.

At this point Christy realized that the field hands were slaves, and she was the daughter of a slave. The place where they were working was the cotton field on a large plantation.

At this point she thought, *Who am I, and where am I?*

The little girl's mother was talking to an old black lady. They were discussing what to fix for dinner. The old lady must be the grandmother of the little girl.

She looked at the little girl and said, "Hello child, how are you?" and asked, "Did you stay out of trouble today?"

The little girl said, "Yes ma'am, I reckon I did."

The old woman smiled and said, "Would you like to tell me about it?"

The little girl said that she played in the wheat fields and chased butterflies. Then she went down to the creek and waded in the water and saw a big fish.

"I tried to catch it to bring home to eat, but it being slimy and all, it got away."

The old lady smiled a big toothless smile and said, "I guess we'll jest hafta eat rabbit, I reckon. Least that way we's not gonna starve."

"Now go help bring some firewood in and git washed up. Now git, girl. I wants to talk to your mama."

The old lady skidaddled the girl outside. As soon as she closed the door, the woman turned to her daughter.

She said, "I hafta tells ya some bad news. The Massa is bad sick. He might die in awhile, and you knows what that means. The son will run the plantation if'n he does. And the devil will be with all of us, that's for sure."

"Oh Lord, I jest hopes the Massa can git well."

The girl came through the door carrying an armload of wood. When the women heard her coming, they both fell silent. They didn't want to upset the child needlessly.

So they talked about the chores and the men who had to do them.

They got their meal fixed and called the menfolk in from the barns. They all sat down at the table to get ready to eat, and the grandmother said grace.

She asked the good Lord to show them a better way of life and prayed for the master to get well.

After dinner the women got all the children off to bed.

There were six children in all, and all were older than the little girl. They all had their own chores to do, and the eldest daughter was working in the big house. She was the house girl for the Mistress of the house.

She liked working in the big house. She talked about all the fine linens and beautiful furniture. She said they had rugs on the floors, and the Mistress had three closets full of beautiful gowns. The beds were so soft and smelled so sweet.

"They smell like a flower garden."

She said everything up there was the way that all people should be able to live.

"It ain't fair that the whites live like that and us negro's live in shacks."

The more the girl worked in the big house, the more she came to hate the white people. It wasn't that she was abused, because she was never abused.

She just thought that no people of any color should be slaves to anyone. And she resented the whites for having all those luxuries when all the black people had were the rags they wore.

They didn't even have their own life. The master owned that.

But the little black girl didn't mind.

The next morning came, and the sun was just coming up. The hands had to get to the fields. The little girl was up too. She wanted to go into the fields with the hands.

She went out the door and just stood and looked around at the beautiful place. The house was elegant and the grounds were well taken care of. The slaves worked in the flower gardens and kept the property around the house beautiful.

The little girl liked what she saw. She said to herself that when she got older she wanted to be in the big house too.

The little girl then realized that someone was calling her, but the name wasn't her name. The voice kept saying, "Christy, wake up."

Then the little girl recognized the voice. She was coming back to the present time, and the voice she heard was her husband.

Christy opened her eyes and looked at Gene.

Gene said to her, "Honey, are you okay?"

Christy said, "I'm fine. Why?"

He said, "Because you were starting to really worry me. You've been asleep for three days, and I was afraid that you weren't going to wake up."

Christy looked up at Gene.

She said, "You know, I had the strangest dream."

Gene asked her to tell him about it, and Christy told him the whole dream right up until the time he woke her up.

Gene said, "Wow, that was some dream. But at least it wasn't a nightmare."

Christy said, "No, it wasn't a nightmare, but it was scary in a way."

Gene said, "What do you mean?"

She told him that in her mind she wanted to stay there, and if he wouldn't have called to her, she felt that she wouldn't have come back.

Gene said, "But you're okay, honey. You're here with me."

She said, "Yes, I am, and it's time to get out of this bed."

Christy got up to take a shower.

Gene went straight to the phone and called Dr. Shaw. He told the doctor about Christy sleeping for three days and said that he was really worried about her.

Gene told the doctor that Christy really liked the dream and wanted to stay where she was. Gene said that he was afraid that she wasn't coming back.

Dr. Shaw told Gene to hang tight and that he and Dr. Whitman would be right over to see Christy.

The doctor then told Gene that if they released Christy to go home, he and Dr. Whitman would see Christy at home and continue her therapy there.

But even after the doctor reassured Gene that everything would be alright, Gene felt that he was losing his wife. He felt totally helpless.

He wanted to fight for his wife—but how do you fight something that you can't see or hear?

After Gene hung up the phone with the doctor, he just sat there with his head hanging. He was praying silently.

"Dear God, please bring her back to me. I'll do anything. Please just bring her back the way she should be so we can get back to our lives."

With that thought in mind, Gene headed down the hall toward Christy's room.

When he turned to go in the door, he saw Christy's medical doctor there talking to her. He told her that they were going to release her to go home.

Gene was happy, but then he had second thoughts.

What happens if I get her home and she slips away to another life and doesn't come back?

Gene thought to himself, *Aren't you being a goof? Just take her home and live day by day.*

Gene's thoughts were broken by the doctor giving Christy her instructions.

He said she had to get plenty of rest and was never to be left alone. She needed someone to help take care of the children too.

Gene spoke up to the doctor and said there was no problem there, because his parents and hers were more than willing to help out.

The doctor said, "Great. Now get her out of here before we change our minds."

He smiled as he said goodbye and headed out the door.

Christy looked at Gene and said, "Are you ready to take me home?"

Gene said, "Absolutely. My lady, I've waited all day for this moment. Now, woman, get your behind in gear before I have to carry you."

They both laughed on their way down the hall.

Christy was headed home to face the unknown.

Gene drove straight to Jake and Ellan's house. Christy wanted to see the children really bad. She simply couldn't wait to hug and kiss them. She missed them so much.

Christy wanted to go straight home, so she told Gene not to stop at the drugstore.

"We'll pick it up later, okay?"

Gene agreed.

When Gene reached the driveway, the children were out playing in the yard. They saw the car and threw down all their toys and ran to the car before it even stopped.

Ellan had to race them to the driveway to keep them out of Gene's way until he got the car parked. Ellan really had her hands full trying to hold both the kids. They wanted to see their mom.

As soon as the car stopped and Christy opened the door, the kids were all over her.

Ellan stood back and watched, thinking a picture is worth a thousand words. She smiled and said to Jake, "I better go and rescue Christy before they kiss her to death. What do you think?"

Ellan went to grab one of the kids, and they screamed and cried. They didn't want to let go of their mommy. They were afraid she would go away again, and they weren't taking any chances.

Christy got the kids into the house, and everywhere she went they followed. But Christy really didn't mind because she missed them too.

She even told them that they didn't need to worry because she was never leaving them again.

Ellan stood by and listened. She was thinking that she hoped Christy was right and that she never had to leave the children again.

But Ellan was worried for Christy and hoped that the doctors could come up with some answers. Ellan was afraid for Christy.

She never told Christy how she felt because she thought Christy was carrying enough of a burden. She had all she could deal with.

Ellan really understood what Christy was going through. She stood by her daughter even in her foul, sarcastic moods.

When Christy was in a bad mood she would call her mother names and make remarks that would really hurt Ellan, but she took the abuse and kept on tending to whatever she was doing.

Sometimes it was hard for Ellan to just stand back and watch what was happening to her little girl.

But all she could do was let Christy know that she loved her no matter what happened.

The evening passed quickly, and Christy was getting the children ready for bed. Ellan offered to help, but Christy refused to let her.

She told Ellan to go sit down and relax.

"You've worked hard enough while I was in the hospital, and this job can be a real chore if you're not used to it."

Christy said to her mom, "You need to relax. So go sit down and prop your feet up. I can handle this."

Ellan smiled and said, "You're right. I am a little tired. I think I'll go watch some TV. If you need me, just yell."

When Christy was finished with the children's bath, she tucked them into bed. They wouldn't let Christy leave the room.

She told them she would tell them a bedtime story.

When she finished the story, she lay down on the bed until they went to sleep. It only took a few minutes, and they were sound asleep.

Christy just lay there and watched the children sleep. She couldn't help but think about what would happen to them if the doctors couldn't help her.

Christy silently wept. She wasn't weeping for herself—she was thinking only of the family and the grief she has caused and might still cause them.

Then Gene crossed her mind, and she felt like her heart was breaking. She loved him so much and knew the pain and agony he was going through.

He's a good man, she thought, *and deserves better.*

She realized that she could never tell Gene what she was thinking. He would be furious.

But she wouldn't have to say anything at all if she just packed her clothes and slipped away in the night. They would all be better off without her.

Christy looked at the children and thought they looked like angels when they were sleeping.

Then she realized that she couldn't slip away like a thief in the night. No matter what happened, they all needed her as much as she needed them.

She vowed to herself that she would do the very best she could.

Christy gently slid off the bed so she wouldn't wake the children. The window in the room was open a little bit, and the night was damp, so she went to the window to close it.

She stood and watched out the window and realized her doctor's appointment was the next morning.

The doctors were coming to the house for Christy's therapy. They thought it would be easier on Christy if she didn't have to travel so much after being in the hospital.

And besides, they needed to start her therapy as soon as possible.

Christy kissed the children and slipped quietly out of the bedroom.

She had the sudden need to be with her husband.

She walked to the living room door and asked Gene if he was ready for bed.

Gene stood up and walked toward Christy. He turned and said good night to Ellan and Jake, grabbed Christy by the hand, and led her back up the stairs.

Halfway up he told her he could hardly wait to be alone with her.

The couple felt like they were on their honeymoon again. They made love and talked awhile, and then made love again.

They told each other how much they missed and loved each other, and cuddled until they both fell asleep.

The next morning came fast. Gene and Christy felt like they had just gone to sleep when it was time to get up already.

Ellan had been up early and had the children fed and out of the way. She didn't want any interruptions when the doctors got there.

Christy had just come downstairs when the knock came on the door. Ellan answered it, and the two doctors stood on the other side smiling at her. She swung open the screen door and asked them in.

When the doctors got inside, Dr. Whitman asked Ellan if this would be a bother to her.

She said, "Absolutely not. I seem to feel better about Christy's therapy this way."

She told them that she thought it might be good for Christy to be at home because she might be more comfortable in her own surroundings.

The doctors both agreed with Ellan as she showed them to the living room.

Gene went upstairs to get Christy.

When she got to the living room, the doctors asked if she minded if they all just sat and talked awhile. They said they thought it might make Christy feel more comfortable and help relieve some of her tension.

They all talked for a long while, and finally Dr. Whitman asked Christy if she was ready to start.

Her reply was, "It's now or never," and she smiled at them.

Dr. Shaw asked Christy, "Are you okay?"

Christy said, "Yes, I'm fine."

Dr. Whitman took over from there.

He said, "Christy, I would like you to tell us about the dream you had while you were in the hospital."

Christy started from the time she was in the open field right up to the time Gene woke her up.

After she had finished, the doctor asked if the dream meant anything to her.

She said no, except that it wasn't like the other dreams she had.

Dr. Whitman asked, "How was it different? Can you explain?"

Christy said, "Yes. I wasn't afraid in the dream. I liked it there. It was a beautiful plantation, and I was a happy little slave girl."

"In my dream I was born into a very poor family. We didn't have anything, but we were all happy. We had a good life there."

Christy asked the doctor why he wanted to know about the dream.

She said it was just a dream and nothing more.

The doctor asked her if she had ever had a dream like this one before.

Christy told him no—never quite like that dream.

Dr. Whitman now asked Christy if she was ready to be hypnotized.

She said yes. She seemed to be quite eager about it for some reason.

Dr. Whitman hypnotized Christy, and she did exactly what he expected her to do.

For some unknown reason, she went right back and picked up the dream where she had left off—almost like she had turned on a switch.

The slaves are all headed to the cotton fields. They're in a hurry because it looks like rain, and they have to get as much cotton picked as possible before the rain comes.

A man is calling someone, but who? He's coming back up the road, and he's looking straight at me.

He says, "Are you deaf or just plain stupid, girl?"

At this point she realizes that her name is Lizzy.

She says, "And a fine name it is too."

The doctor said, "Okay, your name is Lizzy. Lizzy, what are you doing?"

She said, "I'm getting on a wagon and going to the fields with all the hands."

"Lizzy, what exactly is your job in the fields?"

"I carry water to the workers and then the horses. It's so hot out in the sun. There's no shade. I have to go to the big tree. It's so hot I hide there, but if the master finds out he'll beat me."

The doctor said, "I won't tell on you, Lizzy. Does the master beat the slaves a lot?"

"Oh no! Only one time I can remember, and it was the master's son who told him he had no guts."

"Tell me what happened, Lizzy. Can you?"

Lizzy said, "Oh yes, I can tell you."

Lizzy told the doctor that the master was having a big hoe-down. There were lots of people there—some very important people and big plantation owners from around the area.

It was very important to the master that everything went well. He was a very respected man, and most of the people envied him. He had the biggest and best plantation outside of Atlanta. His hands were the best workers in the area.

All his slaves respected him, and he did well by them. He never beat them or treated them badly, and the slaves worked hard for him.

Until this day.

All the people were having a good time. One of the other plantation owners brought one of their slave girls with them. She took a shine to one of the master's young bucks.

Her master caught her talking to him and got angry. He beat her until she bled. She fell to the ground almost blacked out. He hurt her real bad.

The young buck grabbed the man and tried to stop him, and you know what happens when a black man touches a white man.

The white man was raging mad. He wanted to kill the young buck, and the master stepped in to stop him.

He told the white man he would deal with his slaves.

The other man was furious and said that if the master didn't deal with him, he would.

So the master sent one of his older slaves to get the young black boy and take him to the barn.

He said, "I'll deal with him later."

The other slave owner got angry and said, "You have to make an example of him."

My master said, "No! I will deal with it later."

The master's son spoke his piece and told the master he had no guts. He said that he was afraid of the black bastards he owned.

His son shamed my master in front of all his friends.

Now he had to prove he was capable of punishing his slaves if they needed it.

So he went to the barn, and all his guests followed him. They wanted to witness the lashing of the young slave boy.

The master hurt as much as the boy.

When he finished, his eyes were all watery.

He went straight to the big house and didn't come back out.

The party lasted clear into the night.

When all the people went home, the master slipped out to the barn to tell the young man how sorry he was and ask if he could ever forgive him for his stupidity.

The master got on his knees and wiped the blood from the young man's back and sent him home to his mama.

The young man stumbled from the barn, and the master dropped to his knees and asked the good Lord to forgive his weakness.

He stayed in the barn until dawn, still trying to deal with his guilt.

Finally, he slowly made his way to the house.

The doctor is watching Christy as she speaks. He said to her, "How does the master treat you, Lizzy?"

Lizzy said, "The master treats me real well. He likes me a lot. He gives Lizzy candy all the time. But the master's son treats Lizzy real bad."

Dr. Whitman said, "How does he treat you, Lizzy?"

She said, "He called Lizzy to go to the barn. He came to me and grabbed me by the hair. He pulled me down in the hay and ripped my panties off. He touched me where he shouldn't and then he hit me because I didn't do what he wanted. He got on his knees and grabbed my hair again and put my mouth down there. He made me do bad things. Lizzy don't like it, but he hurt me if I don't do what he wants. Then he got real wild and threw me down and he jumped on me. I tried to scream, but he put his hand on my mouth. And all of a sudden, the barn door swings open, and in comes the master. He grabbed the son and told him that he would kill him if he ever touched Lizzy again. The son was real mad. He ran from the barn, screaming at the master. He said, 'You love your niggers more than you ever loved me.' And from that time on, the son never touched Lizzy again."

Dr. Whitman asked Christy if they could move ahead in this life.

Christy said, "Yes, I think so," and continued, "Some time has passed now. Lizzy is growing up, and the son too. The plantation is still the same beautiful place and run the same way. I see the son—he's real nasty. He got mean and hateful to the master and his slaves. He hates the master very much. Lizzy hears him talk to his big brother. He says his father is a coward and that his father would be sorry for treating him the way he does. The son I talk about is the younger of three sons. He believes he is mistreated, even though he is a spoiled brat. He gets everything he wants and always wants more."

The doctor said to Christy, "Lizzy, why do you talk so much about this son?"

Lizzy answered, "Because he scares me."

The doctor said, "Why does he scare you, Lizzy?"

Lizzy said, "Because he would kill to get what he wants."

The doctor said, "And what is it that he wants?"

"She wants the master to die so he can get his share of the plantation," Lizzy said.

The doctor asked, "How old is this son?"

Lizzy said, "Not sure. Maybe sixteen or so. All I know is he thinks he's old enough to run the plantation, but as long as the master keeps hanging on, he's still the boss man."

The doctor said to Christy, "Okay, Christy, enough for today. When I count to three, I want you to open your eyes. One, two, three."

Christy's eyes popped open. She was back in her present life.

The doctor asked, "Christy, do you remember anything that happened?"

Christy said, "Yes, I do. Was it all a dream?"

The doctor said, "What do you think?"

She said, "No. It was real, wasn't it?"

The doctor said, "Yes, Christy, it was real. It was another life."

The doctor told Christy that was all for today and that they would like to continue tomorrow if Ellan didn't mind.

Ellan said it was okay. "Anything to help Christy is okay with me," she said.

After that, the doctors said goodbye and went out the door.

Gene was present during Christy's therapy. He didn't say a word the entire time. He was very confused by it all and was getting to the point where he could hardly handle what was going on.

He felt like he needed to get away for a little while and talk to someone. He went to Christy and asked if she was okay. She said she was fine.

He told her he hadn't seen his mom and dad for some time and that he would like to drive out to the farm.

Christy said, "I think that's a great idea. You need to get out, and your parents will be happy to see you. Go. I'll be fine. I love you, and I'll see you later. Don't worry—just get going."

Gene got himself cleaned up and ready to go. He took his time driving to his parents. He needed some time alone.

He pulled into the lane, and his dad met him at the car. He didn't say anything at first. He just walked over and hugged him.

He said, "How are you, son?"

Gene said, "I'm fine, and I'm sorry I haven't had much time to call you lately."

His father said, "That's okay, son. We understand. Besides, Christy's mom and dad have been calling and keeping us posted on what's been going on."

Gene's father told him how truly sorry he was about Christy. "She's a good mother and wife, and she needs the help of the Lord. You must put Christy and your faith in the hands of the Almighty. That, I believe, is the only way Christy can be saved."

Gene stood with his head hanging. He didn't want his father to see his tear-filled eyes.

Gene said to his dad, "Tell mom I'll see her in a little while. I want to go for a walk and do some thinking."

His father said he would, and Gene walked towards the bungalow.

Gene slowly walked down the path to the bungalow. He stopped in a very familiar grassy area. He sat down and rubbed his hand over the ground. He was thinking about their wedding night and how they had made love in this very spot. He then broke down and cried. His heart was breaking, and he cried until he couldn't cry anymore.

He raised his head and looked up through the trees to the heavens and said,

"Dear Lord, I truly hope You're not too busy to hear me. I know that I'm far from being one of Your perfect human beings. But Lord, I am a true believer, and I believe that whatever is happening to Christy, only You know the answers. And I also believe that You must have a very good reason for it. But Lord, forgive me if I sound selfish. I need her. Please, please, give her back to me. My life is meaningless without her, and I can't stand to see her suffer the way she has. She has been in terrible agony, and I know in my heart that she can't hold on much longer. Please, God, help us."

Gene knelt in the grass and cried his heart out. He was a pitiful sight. His eyes were swollen, and his face was drawn from crying. He finally went limp and fell into the grass. He lay there for hours, crying and praying.

When he was about to leave, a strange feeling came over him. He knew by the feeling that he wasn't alone. He looked around but saw no one. Then he heard a beautiful, heavenly voice.

It said, "Gene, don't worry. Everything will be alright. You put your trust in the Lord, and He will take care of Christy, and you and your family will be fine."

As Gene listened to the last words, the voice faded away. Gene didn't hear anything else. He looked through the trees and weeds to see if anyone was there. He thought someone must be playing tricks on him—and that kind of trick would have been a sick one. But after a while, he realized he was alone in the woods and that he must have been hearing something else entirely.

Gene looked up to the heavens and said, "Thank You, Lord." He then realized that he had heard the voice of an angel.

Gene wasn't really sure what had happened on the way to the bungalow. He just knew that he felt better somehow. At first, he thought it was all the stress, and that crying had released his tension and frustrations. But it was something else—he felt at peace, as if someone had lifted the weight of the world off his shoulders.

He headed back to the house and spent a very peaceful day with his parents. He knew in his heart that it wasn't over by a long shot, but he also knew that everything would be okay in the end.

Gene headed home later in the evening. When he got there, he went straight in to see Christy. She looked up at him with sleepy eyes and said,

"You look fantastic. Did you get some sleep?"

Gene replied, "No, but I did have a nice day. Somehow I feel like everything is going to be alright. I feel deep inside that we're going to beat this thing. We need to be strong."

Gene kissed Christy and sat beside her, taking her in his arms. He held her a long time before saying,

"I really need you, and I love you."

He kissed her again, and they both got ready for bed. They laid in bed and talked until very late.

They decided that it would probably be best if they stayed with Ellan and Jake until Christy was better. But they had to talk it over with Ellan and Jake first. That way, Christy wouldn't have to be with the children alone while Gene was working. And it had to happen soon because Gene had missed far too much work already.

After discussing all that, they finally relaxed and made beautiful love together. They didn't just have sex—they made real love. Afterward, they lay in each other's arms and fell asleep.

But Christy couldn't sleep. She dozed off for a little while but woke up again. Her mind drifted as she thought about the other life. She wondered what it was about Lizzy's life that she liked so much and tried to figure out why it was so different from the other lives she had seen. She thought that Lizzy's life might be the key to her problems.

Her hopes were building, and she thought that if she got back to Lizzy's life, she could find the answers she needed. She grew anxious about her therapy and finally dozed off.

When the sun came up, Christy woke early and got ready to see the doctors. She went to the kitchen, had some coffee, and waited. Soon the doorbell rang. It was the doctors, and Christy ran to open the door.

When Dr. Whitman saw Christy, he was surprised. She looked happy for a change, and the doctor had no idea why.

He asked, "Christy, why are you so bubbly today?"

Christy said, "I'm not really. I just want to get started and get back to Lizzy's life. I want to know what's happening to Lizzy."

The doctors came in, and Christy's therapy began. She relaxed and went into hypnosis right away.

The doctor asked, "Christy, can I talk to Lizzy?"

Christy answered—but it wasn't Christy's voice. It was Lizzy's.

The doctor said, "Lizzy, where are you?"

Lizzy said, with a grin, "Why, I'm in the big house. I'm much older now. I work in the kitchen, and what a fine kitchen it is. I wear a nice clean dress and a new white apron. I look real pretty too. We're fixing food for a big get-together. I've grown to be a young woman. I can see myself in the looking glass. I have a pretty face, my bosoms are very large. I am tall, slim, and very well put together. I must get back to work—Mistress is coming, and I'll get into trouble if I don't hurry."

"Oh no! The Mistress wants to talk to me," Lizzy said, scared. She didn't want to be in trouble.

Lizzy asked, "Mistress, I haven't done anything wrong. Why do you want to see me?"

The Mistress laughed at Lizzy. She said, "You silly girl. You're not in any trouble. I would like for you to be my personal maid. Would you like that, Lizzy?"

Lizzy let out a squeal and said, "I surely would, Ma'am!"

The Mistress said, "Okay, it's settled. Tomorrow morning you start."

Lizzy woke up at the break of dawn. She was really excited about her new duties. She loved beautiful things, and the Mistress had plenty of them. She was being taught how to take care of the nice things and how to do it properly. Lizzy learned very quickly, and the Mistress was very pleased with her.

Lizzy was working where her older sister had worked since Lizzy was a little girl. Soon, Lizzy's sister was sent to another part of the house to work. The sister was angry with Lizzy and said to her,

"I hate you, and you will be sorry you took my position as the Mistress's maid!"

Lizzy had been chosen for the job because the Mistress was tired of the older sister's ways. She said the sister snooped in her things, was very bold, and talked back to the Mistress. The Mistress liked Lizzy because she was very quiet and timid, and she worked hard for her.

One day, Lizzy was outside the Mistress's room in the hallway. She heard the Mistress tell the Master that she was tired of the older sister and thought she needed a good strapping.

The Master asked, "Why?"

The Mistress replied, "She was caught going through my personal things."

The Master said he would put her somewhere she could be watched. Then the Mistress told him that a pair of her diamond earrings were missing. The Master asked if the sister might have stolen them. The Mistress said she couldn't really say—they might just be misplaced.

The Master said that if she did steal them and it could be proven, they would punish her severely, maybe even sell her.

Lizzy ran down the hall to the room where her sister was working. She thought she could warn her sister and help her out of trouble, but the sister was furious and screamed at Lizzy, calling her all kinds of bad names. Lizzy ran out of the room crying. She returned to her own work, trying not to think about her sister's problems.

Lizzy's sister knew exactly why she had been removed from her old job. She had stolen the earrings, and as soon as she could, she snuck them back into the Mistress's bedroom. She dropped them on the floor and slid them under the dresser with her foot, making it look like they had been accidentally dropped.

After a couple of days, the Mistress found her earrings and felt very bad that she had thought the girl had stolen them. She was even sorry that she had moved the sister to another part of the house—but not so sorry as to remove Lizzy. She liked Lizzy and wanted to keep her as her personal maid.

All the while, the doctor was taking notes. He said to Christy,

"Okay, who am I talking to right now?"

Christy replied, "Who do you want to talk to?"

The doctor said, "I need to talk to Christy."

Christy answered, "Okay, Christy will talk to you."

The doctor asked, "Christy, what is it about Lizzy's life that you like so much?"

She said, "I'm not afraid in Lizzy's life. The people treat me well, and I feel safe there."

The doctor said, "But Christy, the people treat you well in your own life too."

She answered, "Yes, but the voices are there, and they scare me. They want to hurt me."

The doctor said, "Christy, what you're saying is that the voices aren't able to scare you in Lizzy's life. Is that correct?"

"Yes," she replied. "The voices can't get there. I don't know why—they just can't. When I'm Lizzy, I'm not afraid of anything. When I'm Christy, I'm afraid of everything. The only thing Lizzy is afraid of is the Master's son, and the Master protects her from him. Other than that, I like Lizzy's life best because the Mistress gives me nice things, like ribbons for my hair and sweet-smelling perfumes. The Mistress is very pleased with me, and that makes Lizzy very happy."

Then the doctor said to Christy,

"Christy, do you remember the responsibilities you have in your life?"

"Yes!" she replied. "When I'm Christy. But when I'm in Lizzy's life, I only know that life."

The doctor said, "Okay Christy, let's go back to Lizzy's life. Can you tell me what's happening in Lizzy's life right now?"

Lizzy is older now, about twenty or twenty-two. She is very happy and has a beau. The Master has given permission for them to be married in the fall.

The doctor asked, "Why in the fall? Why not now?"

The Master said, "Too much work to be done. I don't want the workers distracted until the work is completed. Time is running out, and we will have a short summer. The work comes first. We must do the work."

The doctor studied Christy for a while. He noticed that the more Christy talked, the more she became Lizzy. She spoke like a slave girl from that era—but only in part. For the most part, she was still Christy. It was as if she were torn between two lives and couldn't be complete in either of them.

While the doctor watched, he noticed the look on Christy's face—she looked horrified.

"Christy, what is it? Is something wrong?" he asked.

She didn't answer. She just sat there, staring straight ahead.

The doctor asked again. Still no reply. Finally, he called to Lizzy—and only then did he get a response. Christy was now fully Lizzy, answering only for her.

The doctor asked again, "Lizzy, what's wrong?"

She replied, "It's the Master... he's taken ill. Like before, only I reckon it's worse this time. The doctor is here and tells the Mistress he can't do nothing for the Master... he's dying."

Christy began to cry. She wept, repeating over and over, "My poor Master, my poor Master."

At this point, the doctor felt it was best to bring Christy out of hypnosis. She had enough for one day—he was right. She had been through a lot of strain during the session.

He said, "Okay Christy, when I count to three, I want you to wake up. I also want you to remember everything about what happened to Lizzy. One, two, three."

Christy opened her eyes.

Dr. Whitman asked her if she remembered. She said she did. He said, "Okay, let's talk a little about it."

Dr. Whitman was very concerned about Christy. He felt that if she wasn't happy in her present life, she might revert to Lizzy's life—and they could lose her forever. The doctor needed to find out what was going on inside Christy.

The big question was why she was living two lives—and how it was possible. People who regress to other lives usually move through them quickly, living one life after another. For most, it's like a dream—or a memory that has been stored and forgotten. Like an old movie, or a traumatic event in childhood that they choose to block out. Under hypnosis, those memories can come rushing back.

But Christy was different. She was actually living both lives—almost at will. Dr. Whitman was baffled by all of it.

He then decided to conclude the therapy for the day. He told Christy that they would continue tomorrow if she felt up to it. Christy said that would be fine. The doctors left to return to the office.

CHAPTER
Eight

Losing All Hope

At the office of Dr. Shaw, the two doctors consulted over Christy's case.

Dr. Shaw felt that Christy was using Lizzy's life as a safe haven. Here in Christy's life, she was tormented by the voices and couldn't escape them. But in Lizzy's life, they couldn't get to her because she really wasn't there.

Dr. Whitman said, "So what you're saying is that the voices can't penetrate Christy's mind while she's in Lizzy's life because she is preoccupied with Lizzy and what's happening there?"

Dr. Shaw replied, "Exactly. And as long as we can keep her going with Lizzy's life, it gives us time to try to figure out who the voices are, where they're coming from, and most importantly, why they're here."

Jake and Ellan were sitting at the kitchen table when Gene came in from work. Gene was anxious to find out how Christy's therapy went.

Ellan told him that she would explain everything. She started at the beginning, and Gene and Jake sat quietly, listening. Neither interrupted. They were both astonished by what they were hearing.

Finally, when Ellan was finished, Gene said, "So she likes living in Lizzy's life."

He looked heartbroken. He must have felt like he'd let her down somehow. Ellan tried everything she could to reassure him that it wasn't his fault. She reminded him that Christy had had this problem since she was a child. But no matter how much she said, it didn't seem to make a difference. Gene still felt responsible somehow.

Gene left the kitchen to see Christy. She was resting; the therapy always left her very tired.

He tiptoed into the room where she was sleeping and stood over her, watching. As he looked closer, he realized she was crying in her sleep. He tried to wake her, but she wouldn't respond.

Fear gripped him. He ran to the stairway and called for Jake and Ellan. "Come quick! Something's wrong with Christy. She won't wake up!"

Ellan reached Christy first. She tried everything she could think of to wake her, but nothing worked. Christy remained unresponsive.

Gene ran to the phone to call Dr. Shaw. He explained what was happening. The doctor said they would be there right away and instructed Gene not to leave Christy alone.

Gene hung up and returned to Christy's room. He told Ellan what the doctor had said and that all they could do was wait.

By the time Gene got back to the bedside, Christy had begun thrashing back and forth on the bed. She started screaming—an agonizing scream, like she was in severe pain.

Then, all of a sudden, she stopped. She lay quietly on the bed. A few seconds passed, and then she opened her eyes.

Horrified, she started to cry and reached out for Gene. He grabbed her and sat on the edge of the bed, cradling her in his arms. He tried to soothe her, whispering that it was okay.

She looked up at him with fear in her eyes. "No," she said. "You don't understand. It's not over... it'll only get worse."

By this time, the doctors had arrived. They went straight up to Christy's room.

Dr. Shaw asked her, "What happened?"

She said, "It's Lizzy... she's dead."

Dr. Shaw looked at Dr. Whitman, disbelief written all over his face.

Dr. Whitman asked, "How, Christy? Do you know what happened?"

Christy shook her head. "I really don't know. All I know is... she's dead."

The two doctors just stared at each other. Their theory—that Lizzy's presence in Christy's mind was buying them time to find the key to Christy's problem—had just gone up in smoke. While Lizzy was alive in Christy's mind, she had been giving them precious time.

Dr. Whitman asked, "Christy, are you up for hypnosis?"

Christy said eagerly, "Yes, right away! I... I need to know what happened to Lizzy."

Dr. Whitman proceeded to hypnotize Christy. She cooperated immediately, and within seconds, she was under.

As soon as she went under, the doctor began. "Okay, Christy, who are you?"

She replied, "I'm Lizzy."

"Okay, Lizzy, where are you?"

"I'm in the barn."

"What are you doing in the barn?"

"I'm scared... I'm hiding in a stall."

Dr. Whitman said, "Okay, Lizzy, let's start from the beginning. Tell me why you're hiding in the stall."

Christy scooted up to the head of the bed and curled into a fetal position. She was shaking all over.

She began, "The Master is dead."

After a minute or two, she continued, her voice trembling.

"After the Master died, the two older sons went off to fight in the War Between the States. All of us slaves prayed that the North would win, 'cause if they do, we all will be free… and hope soon too.

"When the oldest sons went to war, it left the plantation in the hands of the youngest son. After the Master died, the Mistress took ill. That left the youngest son to run everything the way he wanted. The Mistress just sat in her chambers, rocking in her chair. She didn't speak anymore. People said she had a sick head and knew nothing since the Master died.

"The son… he was ruthless. Lizzy was scared of him. He was mean-tempered and hurt black folks real bad. He called us niggers and said we were animals. If he didn't get what he wanted, he beat you till the blood ran… and maybe killed you.

"Shortly after the Master died, the young Master came to my shack. He told me to come with him. I said no… he scared me. He got mad, hit me, and knocked me down. Then he grabbed my hair and dragged me to his quarters. When we got there, he slammed the door behind us.

"He went to the fireplace. On the table was a bottle of whiskey. He drank straight from the bottle until it was empty, then threw it into the fire. He turned to me, grabbed my dress, and pulled it until it ripped right off. I tried to cover my body, but he hit me in the face.

"He said, "If you don't want to hurt, you had better do what I tell you."

"He told me to get on my knees and pulled his pants open. I looked at the floor; I didn't want to know what he wanted. It was bad—really bad. He made me do things with my mouth. I'm so ashamed; I want to die. After he finished that way, he threw me on the floor and made me get him excited again.

All the while, he laughed at Lizzy and called me names. He raped me repeatedly. I hurt; Lizzy never did this before, not even with my beau. Lizzy wanted to wait until she married Will before she did anything like this, but she never got the chance to love Will or marry him. The Master found out about him and Lizzy and killed him out of pure spite. He just wanted to keep Lizzy for himself.

Lizzy didn't like it; it hurt, and after the Master was finished with Lizzy, he hit and kicked me and called me "nigger trash." I cried, and he hit me and said he didn't want to see my ugly face there again. I tried to say something, and he hit me real hard alongside my head. I fell back to the floor, and he dragged me to the door and threw me into the hall. He went into his room and slammed the door.

I tried to get to my feet, but I felt like I would black out, and I fell back to the floor. The cool wooden floorboards felt good on my hurt body. I lay there a few seconds to rest and tried to get up again. Then the door opened, and the Master threw all my clothes in my face and told me to get my black nigger ass out of his house.

I got to my feet and ran naked all the way out of the house. The Master had made so much noise that all the other servants were in the entranceway when I ran through. They all saw and knew what had just happened, and I just wanted to die.

I cried all the way back to the shack. Mama was waiting there when I ran in. I looked at my Mama and said, "I wants to kill him. He won't hurt Lizzy no more."

Mama said, "No, child. You must do as he says, or he will be the one who do the killing."

My Mama wiped the blood from my face and tried to comfort me, but nothing seemed to help make me feel the same inside. I just felt hate, and I never hated anyone before. Lizzy hated him because he killed Will—and now, for what he did to me.

Dr. Whitman said, "Lizzy, can you tell me what happened to Will?"

Lizzy said, "Yes, I can. Will was a fine young man. Lizzy and Will grew up together; we were both born on the plantation. As young children, we fought and called each other names. As we grew older, we started to notice different things about each other. He told me once I was a pretty little filly, and I got red in the face and he laughed. From that time on, we became real good friends and then fell in love."

"We wanted to be married," she continued, "so at the end of the war, we could go off and start a new life and family in the free world. Well now, that's not possible, because he's dead. The Master killed him."

The doctor said, "Lizzy, I don't understand. Why did the Master kill your beau?"

Lizzy said, "He hated Will because he loved Lizzy. The Master tormented Will about what he was going to do to Lizzy, and Will got mad. He tried to stay away from the Master, but the Master always followed Will into the barn or into the fields to torment him about me. He was playing a game with Will, and one day he told Will he already made me with child, and Will lost all control. He ran at the Master, and the Master shot him down."

"After Will hit the ground, the Master went to him. He spat on him and laughed as he turned and walked away. After Will died, the Master had two other slaves drag his body to my shack and throw him on the steps. He also sent a message to me. He said that if I didn't do what he said, he would kill me too. That was the time when I swore to my Mama that I would find a way to kill the Master—and kill him with his own gun."

"My Mama pleaded with me not to do anything foolish. She said that he would do to me what he did to Will. Mama said, 'Lizzy, why do you think this way? Child, why don't you just do what he says?'"

"I said, 'No, Mama. I must stop him. He hurt me really bad. Something inside me tells me to do it, and I must. Don't you understand?'"

"Mama said, 'No, child, I don't understand. You can always get better after a beating', but you can't come back from the dead. So please, daughter, do what he wants. I don't want to bury you beside Will.'"

"So, I told Mama okay, I will do what he says, but I won't like it. And now that I'm hiding in the barn and scared out of my wits... I swear, I will kill him before he hurts me anymore."

The doctor said to Christy, "Christy, can you please go on and tell us what happens next?"

Christy continued. She was still very much Lizzy, living Lizzy's life. She said, "I'm still hid in the barn. The barn door opens slowly. It's a young slave boy; he came to fetch me for the Master. I won't go. I know what he wants, and I hide."

The boy pleaded with me. He said the Master will get really mad if I don't do what he wants. I won't go; I slid my body down under a pile of hay and try to hide. Then the barn door swings open with a terrible bang—it shook the whole barn. In comes the Master.

He said to the boy, "Why didn't you do what I told you?" He grabbed him by the neck and threw him out the barn door. He turned around and started to comb through the barn looking for me. I slid further under the hay, and he heard the hay as I moved.

He's coming closer to the stall. I can feel his weight on the hay. He's right over me now and I'm afraid to breathe. He stands still and just listens. The only sound is the beating in my chest. Then, suddenly, I feel a pain in my back. He kicked me, and it felt like he broke my back. He reached down, grabbed me by the hair, and dragged me out of the barn.

All the slaves stood and watched. They, too, were terrified. They knew that if they even made a move towards him, he would kill them. So, they just stood and watched with shame and pity on their faces. I pleaded with him not to hurt me again, and he only hit me and laughed. He was really enjoying all of this, and the more I pleaded, the more he laughed.

Finally, he stopped dragging me. He was making an example of me. I begged him not to hurt me no more. I said I would do whatever he wanted if he didn't hurt me no more. He laughed and said, "I know you will. I own you," and continued to drag me to the house.

When he got to the front porch, I thought he would let me walk up the steps. He didn't. He drugs me up, and the steps hurt my back and hips. When we got inside the house, it was easier for him to pull me on the bare floors, and it didn't hurt as much. Finally, we reached his room. He opened the door and threw me in on the floor.

The door slammed behind us, and he jumped on top of me. He ripped at my clothes until there was nothing left on my body. Every time I tried to move, he hit me. I then closed my eyes and prayed, because I thought I would die right there.

But I felt his hands leave my neck and slip down to my bosoms. He fondled them for a while, like he was enjoying himself, and then he squeezed them with all his strength. I cried out in pain; that gave him great pleasure. From there, he went on down to my belly. He rubbed it and said, "Girl, you're getting as fat as an old pig," and hit me as hard as he could.

She knew she was getting bulky; she was with child. *His child*. But I couldn't say a word. He took his hands down my thigh and ripped my legs open and raped me again and again. He was like an animal. He hurt me; he pushed so hard it hurt my back on the floor. I felt pain all over until he was done with me.

Finally, he came to an end and I thought it was over. But he made me wash him and me so he could start over again. It was a little easier this time; he threw me on the bed and started to have his way. I tried to bear it the best I could. I closed my eyes and tried to think of how nice the linens felt on my naked body. I slid my hand under the pillow and—Lord oh Mighty—I found a gun under there.

I decided right then and there that I was going to use it as soon as I got the chance. I slowly moved my hand out from under the pillow and cocked the gun. He was so busy he didn't even hear it. But when I brought it out to shoot him, he grabbed it from my hand.

He said, "You black bitch, you'll be sorry you tried to do that," and hit me hard on the head. I rolled on my side with pain; there was blood everywhere. When I saw the chance to run, I did. I almost made it to the door when I heard the gun go off and felt a piercing pain in my back. The bullet came straight through and tore a hole in my chest. I fell to the floor and my throat filled with blood.

I can't breathe. Everything is turning black.

Christy laid on the bed, almost lifeless. She was crying softly. The doctor asked what was happening right now.

Christy said, "What can happen… Lizzy is dead, and I watched her die."

The doctors were in disbelief. Christy had actually become Lizzy up until the point of death. Almost as if Lizzy had been living through Christy long enough to tell them what had happened to her. Everything they heard were Lizzy's very own words, right up to the end of her life.

Dr. Whitman said to Christy, "What are you feeling right now?"

Christy replied, "I feel so alone. Lizzy's life is over, and I have nowhere to hide."

The doctor asked, "Why do you want to hide?"

Christy yelled, "The voices! I have no way to hide from the voices. They'll get me now. Lizzy was protecting me. In her life, they couldn't reach me. Now, there's nothing to stop them."

Christy cried in horrible sobs. She was frantic, knowing that the voices would destroy her soon.

The doctor sat quietly for a few minutes. He then asked Christy if she could find out who the voices were, now that Lizzy was out of the way.

Christy sat erect on the bed and screamed, "No! They'll never let you know. If you find out, you might find a way to stop them, and they'll never take that chance."

The doctor said, "Okay then, Christy. Try to contact the voices."

Christy laid back on the bed and relaxed. She closed her eyes and just lay there, very quiet. She looked as though she were sleeping. The doctors looked at each other and thought that Christy had gone to sleep.

They all sat quietly and waited for Christy to do something— but what, no one knew. Ten minutes went by, then fifteen, still nothing. The doctor was about to touch Christy when she sat straight up on the edge of the bed. She stared straight ahead with a strange look on her face. She was in some type of trance.

Dr. Whitman spoke to her, but she didn't hear him. She stood up and headed for the door. Someone was talking to her, and she answered them. She said, "Yes," and went out the door.

When she got to the hallway at the top of the stairs, she said, "Yes, I understand."

Gene ran after her, but the doctor stopped him. He told Gene to let her go and maybe they could find out what was going on inside her head.

Gene got very angry. He said, "No! Are you crazy? They might kill her!"

The doctor, being straightforward, told Gene that they had to let her go so they could find out what they were dealing with. After they discovered the truth, then—and only then—would they be able to help Christy.

Gene looked at the doctor with a pleading face. "They might kill her if we let her go," he said.

The doctor replied, "They're going to kill her anyway if we don't find a way to fight them. So, you see, Gene, we have no choice. We have to let her go."

Gene's face went blank. He was bewildered; he didn't know what to think. But he knew one thing—he had never felt so helpless in his life.

Christy, by this time, had gone down the steps and out the door to the porch. On her way through the hall, at the bottom of the steps, she stopped and picked up her car keys.

Christy walked down the steps to the driveway. She walked right past Ellan and Jake, seemingly looking right through them. She didn't even notice the children playing in the yard. She got to the car and got in. She sat behind the steering wheel, both hands tightly gripping it. She just stared out the windshield, almost like she was waiting for something.

A few minutes went by, and she started the car. But then, all of a sudden, she began screaming. "No! I won't, I won't! What do you want from me? I won't go!"

After that, she slumped over the wheel and began to cry hysterically.

Gene couldn't stand any more of this. He ran to the car and opened the door. He grabbed Christy and pulled her from the car. She was crying so hard, her knees were weak, and she almost fell. Gene caught her just as she was about to hit the ground. He knelt in the grass and held Christy, trying to calm her down.

After Gene got Christy to her feet, he helped her back to the house. Ellan led them into the living room, and they all sat down with Christy. Gene tried to get her to talk, but she only cried. After a while, she stopped crying and just stared into space. She wouldn't respond to anything they said to her.

Gene was really worried. He asked the doctor what was wrong with her and why she was like this. The doctor replied that in her mind, she was off somewhere else—a safe haven for her. Evidently, the voices couldn't reach her there. She had chosen to be in her own little world, and now that she was there, there wasn't much anyone could do for her.

Gene got angry. He said to the doctor, "What the hell are you talking about? You mean you won't even try to bring her back?"

The doctor said, "Please try to understand, Gene. We might be able to help her, but we would have to put her in an institution to accomplish anything. She's too far gone now."

Gene lost all control. He got right in the doctor's face and screamed, "Never! I promised her that would never happen, and it won't!"

The doctor backed away and simply shook his head. Dr. Whitman turned to Dr. Shaw, and they both stood up to leave.

Gene stopped them. "Where the hell do you think you're going?" he demanded.

Dr. Shaw spoke up. "Gene, if you don't let us take her with us, there's nothing we can do. If you change your mind, you know where to reach us."

The two doctors went out the door. Gene followed them to the door and watched as they drove off. He thought about all the hope they had, watching it drive away. But there was nothing he could do—he had promised his wife he wouldn't let them put her away, and he fully intended to keep that promise.

Days had gone by, turning into weeks, and weeks turning into months. And Christy still hadn't come back from wherever she might be. They had come to believe that she must be safe there; otherwise, she would have been back by now.

Ellan and Gene had been taking care of her and the children. Ellan had to bathe Christy and feed her to keep her alive. Christy wouldn't respond to anything—she just sat and stared. All the food Ellan could get into her was liquids, and even that was difficult. But Ellan was very patient with Christy. Even if it took hours, she made sure her daughter ate.

Ellan's heart broke for the children. They asked, *"What happened to our mommy?"* and no one knew the answers. They wanted to know why she didn't kiss and play with them. They asked why she didn't tuck them into bed. Sometimes they said, *"Our mommy doesn't love us anymore."* Ellan tried to explain but couldn't. She just told them their mommy was sick, and they went back to what they were doing.

Gene was always glad when the children went to Ellan with their questions. He couldn't handle all the things they came up with. They were normal, healthy children, and what one didn't think of, the other did. Gene, having questions of his own, couldn't quite deal with it, so he let Ellan and Jake handle it, and he was surely thankful they were there.

But even so, Gene felt forsaken. He was beginning to think that everything he believed in had turned sour.

Ellan was getting the children ready for bed, and like every other evening, the children wanted to go see their mommy. Then, they started with all their questions. Gene just couldn't handle it anymore; he felt like he couldn't go on. He decided to sit on the porch, take in the evening air, and be alone for a while.

As he sat on the swing, he looked up at the stars and thought how beautiful they were. Then he found himself thinking about their wedding night and the stars in the sky that night. He broke down and cried. He missed Christy so much. He needed her to talk to and be in his life. He felt like he couldn't go on.

Finally, he wept and said, *"Lord, have You overlooked us, or have You just forgotten about us? I know You're extremely busy, but I don't believe You would be too busy to hear the prayers of someone who has as much faith as we do. I believe that when the time is right, You'll come to us. But Lord, I don't think I can go on, and I pray not for me, but for Christy. Please God, help us before it's too late for her."*

After that, Gene fell to his knees and cried his heart out. He stayed out there for a long time. It was around midnight when he finally went into the house. He went up to Christy's room and sat on the edge of her bed. When he saw her, he cried again and held her hand. He prayed again.

Gene really felt like he was losing touch with reality. He reached up and kissed Christy on the lips and told her he loved her, then started to get up off the bed.

As he turned away from Christy, he felt something touch his arm. He turned back, and Christy was lying there, smiling at him.

She said, *"Honey, what's wrong? Why are you crying?"*

Gene couldn't believe his eyes. He said, *"Honey, you're okay."*

Christy said, *"Of course I'm okay. Why?"*

Gene knew by the way she was talking that she didn't know what had happened. And he was right—she didn't remember anything. She didn't even know what day or month it was. She had just picked up where she left off all those months ago.

But one thing she did know was that she was really hungry.

Gene said, *"You're hungry? Well, I can take care of that. Don't move—I'll be right back."*

Gene ran down the steps. Jake followed him to the kitchen to see what was wrong. Gene went to the refrigerator and got all kinds of food out. He made a three-layer sandwich and fixed some homemade soup that was left over from supper.

Ellan and Jake just stood and watched. They were thinking, *Gene has gone completely mad—or starving.*

Ellan finally said to him, *"Are you going to eat all that after the big meal we had? Or are you feeding an army somewhere we don't know about?"*

Gene, in all his excitement, didn't even think to tell them about Christy. He dropped everything he was doing and ran over to Ellan. He grabbed her in his arms, picked her up off the floor, and started to dance around the kitchen.

Ellan said, *"For God's sake, Gene, what's got into you?"*

He put Ellan on the floor and smiled. He said, *"Christy. Christy has gotten into me. She's hungry, and I'm going to feed her."*

Ellan was shocked. She said, *"How dare you make light of the situation! How dare you!"*

Gene said, *"No, I'm serious. She's hungry. Go see for yourself."*

Ellan burst into tears, and she and Jake ran as fast as they could up to Christy's room. They got to the door and stopped to catch their breath. They seemed a little reluctant to go in, almost like they were afraid of being disappointed. But they looked at each other and turned the corner.

And there, on the edge of the bed, sat Christy—bigger than life itself.

Christy looked at her mom and dad. She said, *"What's wrong? You both look like you've seen a ghost."*

Ellan said, *"Honey, are you okay?"*

Christy said, *"Why does everyone keep asking me that? Yes, I'm okay."*

Ellan said, *"Christy, do you know what day it is?"*

Christy said, *"Yes, it's Tuesday, and I talked to the doctors today."*

Ellan said, *"No, honey, you haven't seen the doctors for months."*

Christy couldn't believe what she was hearing. She knew her mother would never lie to her about something like that, so she knew it was the truth.

Just then, Gene came into the room with a tray of food. He saw the look on Christy's face and knew she realized what had happened.

She asked him, *"Gene, how is it possible to live from day to day and not even know you exist? Have I gone mad?"*

Gene put down the tray and took Christy in his arms. He said, *"Don't worry about all that. We have you back, and that's all that matters."*

After they talked for a while, Christy ate her food. She asked Ellan where the children were. Ellan told her they were in bed—it was late. Christy said she would peek in on them before she went to bed. She decided to put all that had happened behind her and see what the morning would bring.

The next morning was a glorious one. Christy got up early and went to the kitchen to make coffee. Soon, the whole family was up.

The children came racing down the steps and into the kitchen. When they saw their mother at the stove, they squealed and ran to her. They both tried to jump up and hug her. She made it easy for them and bent over to kiss and hug each one of them. They were so happy to see her.

It was a sight to behold. Ellan sat at the table with tears in her eyes.

All of a sudden, Sammie pulled away from her like she had pinched him or something. He said sarcastically, *"Why wouldn't you talk to me and sissy? What did we do to make you not love us anymore? Were we bad or something?"*

Christy grabbed him and said, *"Oh no, honey. You weren't bad. It was me. I was sick or something. I'm so sorry. I won't do it anymore, I promise."*

Christy thought that she would like to explain, but how do you explain something you know nothing about? She didn't even know herself what happened, so how could she tell them?

She sat down at the table and tried to explain as best she could. After she was finished talking to the children, they were happy. They all ate their breakfast and tried to get on with their lives.

A few days have gone by, and Christy has been very normal. She's been taking care of the children and trying very hard to get back into her routine as a mother and wife. It really wasn't difficult for her, because she was good at almost everything she did. She had always been a good wife and mother.

And after all they'd been through, Gene and Christy were still very passionate with each other. That made the "wife" part come very easily. The two of them were still very young at heart. They would take an afternoon and sneak off to be alone. They acted like newlyweds when they were alone.

They made passionate love and then just fooled around. They were happy when they wrestled with each other, and Gene always got the best of Christy in the end. Before she admitted defeat, she teased Gene into another round, which always led to them making love again. Gene would get worn out from all that, and Christy would giggle and call him an old man. He'd respond, *"I'll show you who's old!"* and they'd wrestle some more.

Finally, wearing themselves out, they would just lie together, enjoying the closeness of their bodies, and fall asleep. They wished things would stay this way—forever.

CHAPTER
Nine

The Final Chase

A month had gone by now, and nothing had happened. Everyone, including Christy, was very happy. They all thought it might finally be over.

Gene returned to work steadily, and they all lived like one big happy family. Gene and Christy gave up their house and moved in with Jake and Ellan. They really couldn't afford not to; all the bills had piled up and needed attention. Gene tried to take care of things, but with all the time he had missed at work, it was impossible.

Thank goodness he had a sympathetic boss, or he wouldn't even have a job. With a little time, things would get back to normal, and life wouldn't be so tough. Living with Christy's parents wasn't as expensive. They shared the utilities and food bills. They didn't have to pay rent, which was a big savings in itself. They figured that within a couple of months; the bills would be caught up. With all of Gene's overtime, they might even have money to spare.

The alarm clock went off. It was time for Gene to get ready for work. Christy woke up with a severe headache, so Gene packed his own lunch and prepared to leave. Christy went to the door with him and kissed him goodbye.

He turned and was gone. After a few seconds, he came running back in. He told Christy it was a cold September morning and he needed a jacket. Christy ran up the steps to their room and got his work jacket out of the closet.

"I'm coming," she said.

When she got back to Gene, she asked if her mother was awake.

Christy said, "No, why?"

Gene replied, "I thought you were talking to someone."

She said, "I was—I was talking to you."

"Oh, I didn't hear you. What did you say?" he asked.

Christy said, "Nothing, I just answered you."

Gene looked at her and knew what had happened. He got worried—and with good reason. The voices were calling her again. Gene had to go to work, and Christy went back to lie down, her head splitting. She fell back asleep.

Ellan got up with the kids and fed them their breakfast. She then went to check on Christy. Christy was still asleep. Ellan sat down on the bed beside her and shook her to wake her.

Christy rolled over and said, "Good morning, Mom."

Ellan asked if she was going to sleep all day.

Christy asked, "What time is it?"

Ellan told her it was noon.

Ellan asked if she felt okay.

Christy said she was just tired. "After I get a shower, I'll be alright. Go ahead downstairs," she told Ellan. "I could really use a good cup of coffee."

"Coming right up," Ellan replied.

Ellan left the room and stopped by her own bedroom to clean up a little before going downstairs. After she finished, she began going down the steps when she heard Christy talking to someone. Ellan assumed it was one of the kids—they had been wanting to wake her all morning.

But when Ellan got to the kitchen, she looked out the window and saw both children in the yard with Jake. Ellan ran back up the stairs and went into Christy's room. Christy was in the shower now. Ellan tiptoed over to the door to see if she could hear anything. Everything was quiet, so Ellan went over and sat down on Christy's bed.

Ellan wanted to be very careful not to upset Christy, but she had to find out who she was talking to. When Christy came out of the bathroom, she had a towel over her head. When she looked up and saw Ellan, she was startled; she didn't expect anyone in the room.

Christy snapped at Ellan, "What are you doing, snooping around in my room?"

Ellan was shocked by her reaction. She tried to explain, but Christy wouldn't hear a word she said. She just mumbled to herself and continued to get dressed, throwing clothes all over the room. She was raging and talking to someone else.

Ellan got scared and left the room to get Jake. When the two of them returned, Christy was smiling and said, "Hi, Dad. What's up?"

Ellan looked at Jake in disbelief. Jake just shrugged his shoulders and said, "Hi," to Christy. Then he asked, "Are you coming down soon? The kids want to play with you."

Christy told him to lead the way, and down the steps they went.

When they got to the door, she ran out to see the children. Ellan told Jake what had happened upstairs. Jake looked at Ellan as if he couldn't believe what he was hearing.

Ellan, frustrated, said to Jake, "I know what I heard, and I'm not crazy, so don't look at me as though you think I am."

Jake replied, "Honey, I don't think you're imagining things. I, too, am trying to figure out what's going on. I hope she's not having a relapse." He added that they would have to watch her closely today and not leave her alone with the kids for too long.

Ellan and Jake didn't have to worry for very long, because Christy came back into the house about fifteen minutes later. She went straight to her room. After a short while, Jake went to check on her and found her back in bed. He quietly slipped back down the steps.

Both he and Ellan were at the point that neither of them knew what to do, so they decided to just keep an eye on her until Gene got home.

Christy slept all day without incident. Ellan went to check on her several times during the day, and everything was quiet. Christy didn't even move. She lay in the same position all day.

When Gene got home, it was around six o'clock in the evening. Ellan met him at the door and told him the news. Gene went to Christy's room and tried to wake her.

She screamed at him, "Go away! I want to sleep."

Gene said, "Honey, you've slept all day."

Christy opened her eyes and glared at him. "I know I've slept all day, and I'm going to stay in bed until I'm damn good and ready to get up. Now get the hell out of here." She reached for the nightstand and grabbed the clock radio.

She threw it at Gene. He ducked, and it slammed into the door. Ellan and Jake heard the crash and ran up the steps to see what happened.

Christy saw them and asked, "What the hell are you looking at?"

Jake tried to answer, and she threw a lamp at him. The lamp hit Ellan on the forehead and cut her badly. Blood splattered on the door and walls. Ellan fell to the floor, and Jake pulled her to her feet and got her clear of the flying objects.

He went back to the room to see if he and Gene could do anything to calm Christy down. It was no use. She was so out of control that they both left the room and closed the door behind them.

The two went to get Ellan and tend to her cuts. They took her down to the kitchen. Gene called his parents to see if they could come and get the kids. Gene explained the situation, and his mother said they would be there right away.

Gene went back to the kitchen to see how Ellan was. She was still bleeding, and Gene said, "You may have to go to the doctor and get stitches."

Ellan told Gene, "I'm not leaving until I know that Christy is alright."

About an hour later, Gene's parents arrived. Gene and his dad went upstairs to see if they could do something with Christy. They stood in the hall and listened. Christy was talking to someone.

She said, "Yes, I will. Don't rush me. I'm almost ready."

Gene opened the door a little crack, just enough to see inside. Christy saw him. She screamed, "You bastard! Get out! Stop snooping and staring at me. Go away! I hate you!"

Gene looked at his dad. He had tears in his eyes. He told his dad that he knew what he had to do. They both went down the steps.

Gene went to the phone and called Dr. Shaw. He told the doctor what had been going on. The doctor said, "What can we do?"

Gene replied that they knew what to do. Dr. Shaw told Gene that they would take care of the arrangements and would be there as soon as they could. Now, all Gene had to do was tell Ellan and Jake—and he knew that they would take the news very hard.

Gene hung up the phone and stood there for a long while. He knew that Ellan and Jake weren't going to be happy with what he had to tell them. He took a deep breath and slowly moved toward the kitchen.

When Gene got to the kitchen door, he stopped. His mom and dad were on one end of the table, and Ellan and Jake were on the other. Gene just stood there, staring at the floor. He couldn't bring himself to give them the bad news, but he knew he had to. The doctors would be there soon, probably with an ambulance to take Christy to the institution.

Gene staggered to the table to sit down. When he reached it, he almost fell off the chair as he tried to sit. He burst into tears. His mom went to console him, and he cried like a baby in her arms.

After he got himself together to the point that he could talk, he pleaded to Ellan and Jake, "Please... don't hate me for what I've done."

Ellan said, "Gene, we could never hate you. You're like a son to us."

Gene said to her, "After I tell you the news, I'll understand if you do."

Jake asked in a very stern tone, "What news?"

Gene dropped his head and tried to explain.

Gene started by saying, "You know, I love Christy with all my heart, and when she's like this, I can't stand to watch her. I'm so afraid that she is going to hurt herself... maybe even one of the children. Oh! I know she wouldn't do anything in the world to put them in danger in her right mind, but I have come to the realization that she is being controlled by another source. Until we find out what the other source is, we can't help her. She's in danger, and so is everyone around her. I'm really concerned with the well-being of the children. I believe the adults in this house can deal with Christy. My main concern is trying to keep Christy from destroying herself. That's why I called the doctor. They're on their way as I speak, and they're going to take Christy to the hospital."

Ellan jumped up from the table and said to Gene, "Don't you mean the institution?" She was angry, and Gene felt like his world was collapsing.

He turned to leave the room, but Jake stood up, put his hands on Ellan's shoulders from behind her, and told her to sit down. He called to Gene to stop and turn around. Gene did as Jake said.

When Gene turned around, he looked drained. He had been crying silently. His face was tear-stained, and his eyes were swollen. Jake went to Gene, put an arm around his shoulders, and led him back to the table to sit down. Gene sat there with his head in his hands. He couldn't look at anyone. He felt he had betrayed all of them, especially Christy.

Jake stood by Gene and said, "Gene, I know what you've been through. I can understand why you called the doctor. Christy needs help—the kind of help we can't give her. And in your heart, you, and all of us in this room, know that you did the right thing. All we can do is pray that they can help."

Even after Jake spoke to Gene, he didn't seem to feel any better. He could only think of the promise he gave his wife. He felt as though he'd let her down. She trusted him, and he betrayed that trust.

A knock came at the door. Gene went to answer it. Dr. Whitman and Dr. Shaw were standing on the porch. They both looked very gloomy. The task they had to do wasn't easy for them either. They had discussed the situation on the way over and knew the trauma the family would experience when they saw their loved one being taken away. All the doctors could do was reassure them that they would do everything humanly possible to help Christy.

As the doctors were talking to the family, a loud crash came from upstairs. Gene ran up the steps, two at a time, to get there. When he reached Christy's door, she started screaming.

Gene tried to open the door, but Christy had it barricaded. He couldn't even budge it.

Jake came up, and Gene told him what she had done. They tried to figure out another way into the room. The two men went to the porch roof. Gene crawled out the window onto the roof. From there, he had to climb the latticework attached to the side of the house.

Jake warned him, "Be careful. The wood is very old and weak."

Gene started to climb, reaching for the lattice, but when he put his weight on it, the wood pulled away from the house. Gene dangled in midair. Jake knelt down and tried to grab him, but missed. Gene fell into the bushes below.

Jake screamed for the doctors, and they all rushed down to see if Gene was okay. When they reached him, he hadn't moved. He had hit his head on the porch railing and was unconscious. When he came around, he had a small cut on his head, but he said he was fine. All he cared about was Christy. They had to figure out another way to get to her.

Christy was still screaming and shouting at someone in her room. "I won't go!" she yelled. But after a few seconds, she seemed to give in to whoever she was talking to.

All the men were at the bedroom door, trying hard to get in. After a while, the room grew quiet. Dr. Shaw said, "Maybe she went to sleep." They stood in the hall discussing their options for getting to Christy.

Ellan came running up the stairs, too excited to speak. Once she caught her breath, she told Gene that she had seen Christy climbing down the lattice. She said Christy then got into the car and drove away.

"I'll catch her," Gene said.

Jake replied, "Not without me."

They ran to Gene's pickup truck and headed out the road. Soon, they met the ambulance at the main road. Gene had the ambulance stop and spoke with the driver. The driver said the car he saw was headed toward the highway.

Back at the house, the doctors notified the police and explained Christy's condition. The police were very concerned for everyone's safety and put out an all-points bulletin on the vehicle Christy was driving. Meanwhile, the doctors gave Ellan something to calm her down, and Gene's mother stayed at the house until they heard from the men.

Gene and Jake reached the highway. Immediately, they spotted signs of Christy's path. On the northbound side, a man was standing by the guardrails. He said a woman had run off the road, describing Christy's car in detail.

Gene told the man he would send help when he reached a phone, but it wasn't necessary. A police cruiser had already pulled off to talk to him. Gene was thankful he didn't have to waste time calling the police himself.

By the way the man talked, Christy was traveling at a high rate of speed. Gene feared he might not be able to catch her. All he could do was keep driving north, hoping she might run off the road just enough to stop her without harming herself or anyone else. Jake sat quietly, hanging on, silently praying the whole way.

Gene drove a few miles north on the highway. They came upon a ramp—there was no mistaking that Christy had come this way. Several cars were piled up in the median strip. One car lay on its side.

Gene carefully maneuvered through the tangled mess and continued north in pursuit of Christy. He prayed to God that no one had been seriously hurt in the accident. Then he thought that he must have been meant to find Christy—she was leaving a trail of wrecked automobiles for them to follow.

For Gene and Jake, it was a grueling task. The two men didn't dare stop, for if they did, it might be too late for Christy.

All they could do was keep traveling north at a high rate of speed, hoping to catch up with her.

Soon, the men came to the parkway. Christy went east. Traffic on the parkway was usually heavy, but tonight there didn't seem to be any tie-ups. Traffic was moving smoothly. Though, there were clear signs that Christy had come this way. The men continued toward Pittsburgh.

Christy had been traveling north without even realizing she was in the car. She was in a trance. The only thing she was aware of was the voice urging her on. The voice kept telling her to drive faster. She tried to fight it, but the power the voice had over her was too strong. She unwillingly obeyed.

Occasionally, when she struck the side of another car, she briefly returned to reality—but never for long. The voice took over again, and she followed its instructions exactly. The more she obeyed, the stronger and more overpowering the voice became.

Christy approached the hill before the tunnels. Traffic began to get heavier. She drove down the berm, scraping her car on the guardrails on one side and sideswiping cars on the other. Truckers using two-way radios tried to warn the drivers at the bottom of the hill.

Just before Christy reached the tunnels, police sirens blared from every direction. Officers had been in hot pursuit since the first accident on the highway, but they had just missed her. She made it to the tunnels before they could pull her over. Along the way, she hit a car on the front fender while weaving through traffic.

It seemed as if the force driving her had other plans for Christy. Despite all the accidents she caused, she wasn't hurt in any of them—almost as if some unseen force was protecting her.

Christy got through the tunnels. By this point, her car was literally falling apart; pieces were flying everywhere. The police were right on her bumper, but Christy had no idea they were even there. She was following her instructions.

The voices told her: "When you get through the tunnels, get into the far left-hand lane and follow it all the way around. Break through the barricades and drive across the bridge."

Christy did exactly what she was instructed to do.

The police following Christy were in disbelief. The bridge she was traveling on had not yet been completed. It had been nicknamed *The Bridge to Nowhere*. Several police cruisers flanked her car, but she didn't even know they existed. She continued driving straight through the barricades.

The officer on the right radioed the one on the left, warning them to be careful. They were almost at the end of the bridge and admitted they didn't think there was any hope. They had come to believe that the girl in the car "wanted to commit suicide." Of course, they were wrong—but they had no way of knowing that. All they could do was stay with her and hope she stopped before the end of the bridge.

It was certain death if she didn't. The drop was about sixty feet into the river below. Even if she survived the plunge, she would likely drown before anyone could reach her. The police had already contacted the Coast Guard, who replied, "We are at the river and will be there in only minutes." Just then, they saw the rescue boats approaching.

Gene and Jake were right behind the police. The officers were so focused on Christy that they didn't notice the car pursuing them at high speed. At this point, Gene didn't care. All that mattered was reaching Christy.

A wall of police cruisers blocked the road, and Gene couldn't get around them—until finally, one car veered to the right, allowing him to squeeze through. Once past, the officer in that cruiser got on the PA system, ordering Gene to pull over, insisting it was a police matter. Gene ignored him and kept driving. Soon, he finally caught a glimpse of Christy's car.

Christy remained in a trance. The farther she drove, the stronger the voices' control over her mind became—almost as if they were determined to end her life. The closer she got to the edge of the bridge, the faster the voices demanded she go.

The police assumed that perhaps at the end of the bridge, Christy would stop—and the chase would finally be over. But only seconds later, they witnessed Christy's car leave the edge of the bridge and go airborne.

CHAPTER
Ten

A Miracle In The Making

From this point on, everything seemed to move in slow motion. They all felt helpless; all they could do was watch as the car plunged into the cold, dark river. Gene saw Christy's car go over the edge. He screeched to a stop and, with Jake, ran to the edge of the bridge. All they could see was the red glow of her taillights. Gene dropped to his knees, crying, repeating over and over, "Christy, why? My God, Christy, why?" Jake knelt beside him, trying to console him, though his heart was breaking as well. From that moment on, time seemed to stand still.

The Coast Guard was almost at the spot where Christy's car had gone under. The river was dark, and the city lights reflected off the water. There was no sign of the car. Gene prayed, waiting for his wife to surface, but she did not. The Coast Guard arrived at the crash site, divers ready to enter the water—when, all of a sudden, the sky lit up.

The sight was something one could only dream about. It was magnificent. The sky, totally dark with no moon in sight, seemed to open, and rays of light poured down onto the river exactly where Christy's car had sunk. The light was cool and soothing, almost heavenly.

Everyone who had come to witness the death of a young woman now witnessed something entirely different. The crowd stared at the opening in the sky, not with fear, but with awe. This was a *miracle in the making*. And after what happened next, there could be no doubt—a miracle it was.

Through the opening in the clouds, a glowing light shone, and within it were the images of two angels. They floated down to the river, submerging themselves into the water. The river took on a warm, radiant glow, pale blue and green. For a few seconds, spectators could make out the outline of the car, rocking gently with the current.

The crowd stood frozen, some in shock, some in silent reverence, all realizing they were witnessing a miracle in progress. Soon, the two figures emerged from the water, Christy held safely between them. They rose slowly into the heavens, entering the hole in the clouds. The sky closed around them, and everyone remained still, staring upward. No one moved for a long, silent moment.

They just stood and stared. Some got down on their knees and prayed. The Lord's Prayer could be heard, and people held rosary beads in their hands. People of all religions knew, without a doubt, that this was the work of Almighty God.

The police had gathered at the edge of the bridge. Between them, they didn't know what to put in their reports. They all knew that no one would believe a story like this. One officer suggested they locate the family of the woman in the car. Jake overheard the conversation and spoke up, saying that he was the girl's father and pointing to Gene, saying that he was her husband.

The officer turned to look at Gene, then back at Jake. He apologized to Jake, saying how sorry he was that his daughter had gone into the river. He asked Jake to sit in the police car and opened the door for him. After Jake sat down, the officer went to get Gene. He spoke softly to Gene—Jake couldn't hear the words, but guessed the officer was saying the same things to Gene that he had just said to Jake. The officer returned to the car, and Gene followed him. He opened the door for Gene and closed it behind him. The officer and his partner sat in the front seats.

The men in the car were quiet for some time. The officers didn't want to push them—they understood the pain they were feeling. After a few minutes, Gene began to speak, telling the police the whole story from the very beginning. As he spoke, a crane was on its way to pull Christy's car from the river. The police needed to confirm that Christy's body was still inside. They all thought they were dreaming. There was no other explanation for what they had seen—but they knew it had to be impossible. And yet, they had all seen the same thing.

Christy was very cold and shivering. She opened her eyes. Everything around her was white, clean, and beautiful. She was floating, surrounded by angels. One of the angels approached her.

Christy asked, "Am I dead?"

The angel touched Christy's forehead, gently rubbing her hand across her head and down around her cheek. She lifted Christy's head and said, "No, child, you're not dead."

Christy said, "But I don't understand. If I'm not dead, then where am I? And how did I get here?"

The angel told her to lay back and relax, and promised she would explain.

Christy rested her head and thought to herself, *I've never felt anything so soft in my life.* She raised her head to look around and was astonished. She was lying on a bed of clouds. Beneath the clouds stood four pillars, white with gold braids, ribbons, and bows. Christy couldn't believe her eyes. She had never seen anything so magnificent in her life. Everything around her looked like something out of a fairy tale.

Christy thought that if she wasn't dead, then she surely must be dreaming. She studied everything around her. She watched the clouds as they floated by. Christy imagined them like big rolls of fluffy white cotton.

Then she looked through the opening directly in front of her. Off in the distance, she saw something so far away she could hardly make it out. She sat up and focused her eyes. Slowly, the picture became clear. She was breathless. She was seeing something that some people would never see. At that moment, she thought she must be in heaven—or at least very close.

The image through the clouds revealed the gates of heaven. It was breathtaking—a golden stairway leading into golden gates. Angels hovered around the entrance. Some were blowing trumpets, while others guided people through the gates as they opened. Their feet never touched the ground; they floated gracefully to the stairway, then walked up the steps and entered heaven.

Christy lay back, waiting her turn. She figured that if she was this close, she surely must be dying. She stayed there for a long while before the angel spoke again.

"Do you feel better now?" the angel asked.

Christy nodded. "Yes… but I don't seem to understand. If this is not heaven, then where am I, and why am I here?"

The angel smiled. "Try to relax, Christy. I'll start from the beginning and explain everything—starting from when you were a little girl."

The angel began to tell Christy her whole life story, speaking in a soft, heavenly voice. It was easy for Christy to relax and listen to every word.

"Christy," the angel said, "in the beginning of time, God created the heavens and the earth. As the Creator, He decided that all His creations needed care. He then made man. For each man and woman, He created an inner being. Each of these beings is made of both good and evil. These inner beings have names; they are known as the spirit or soul. God made only so many souls, and each soul has a duty to fulfill.

"Until its duty is complete, a soul stays on Earth. When a person dies a sudden or tragic death, the soul slips out of that body and enters the next person who is born. The soul remains with that person, trying to fulfill its duty. In many cases, the person dies before the soul's work is finished, so the spirit must stay until the job is completed."

Christy interrupted, "I understand all that, but what does it have to do with me?"

The angel looked at her kindly. "Everything, Christy. You have experienced many things you do not understand. If you give me a chance, I will explain."

"Christy, when you were born, you were different in many ways," the angel said. "You heard voices—from someone who wasn't visible to you. Then you began to see things that a child your age couldn't possibly understand. You tried to tell your parents, but they thought you had a very active imagination. They just said, 'Yes, dear,' and let it go at that.

"But as you grew older, you realized something was very wrong. You lost control of your life at times. The voices took over and demanded things from you that could have destroyed you. In your mind, the voices were very real. In the beginning, they controlled you easily, at their will. But as you grew older and stronger, you began to fight back.

"The voices you heard were actually only one voice. Your soul made it sound like multiple voices, thinking that the more voices you heard, the quicker you would obey—and that fear would drive you to certain disaster. It almost worked—until the day we connected with your soul. You'll remember that day very well.

"Do you remember the crash on the highway? The one where you saw the woman in the middle of the two lanes?"

Christy nodded. She studied the angel's face for a moment. "It was you," she said softly. "You were the woman on the road, and I had to slam on the brakes to avoid hitting you. You could have had us killed—all those people in the crash who died. It was your fault."

The angel shook her head gently. "No, Christy, you don't understand. Listen closely."

"The accident was exactly as it was supposed to happen. Those people's names were already on the list to enter heaven. You were the only one who was not meant to die that day. Your soul knew of the accident and drew you to the scene. It wanted you to die so it could successfully enter another life and avoid the spirit world one more time. But it was very disappointed—your guardian angel, me, was there to protect you.

"As with all the other times, you could have died. But I couldn't intervene until the very end. When your spirit started to lift from your body, that was the moment I had to bring you back. If the timing hadn't been right, your soul would have left your body, and you would have been left on Earth without a soul—that would have been catastrophic. Only the Lord knows what might have happened then. God gave us our instructions, and we did not question His authority. We were there from the very first time—when you were only four years old, in the water."

Christy's eyes widened. "Yes, I remember that very well. My head was under the water—I needed air. I couldn't breathe. My chest and lungs felt like they would burst. My hair caught in some rocks and debris at the bottom of the creek. The water was shallow, but I couldn't get my head up far enough to get any air. I was drowning.

"I thought I saw angels that day, but later I thought I must have imagined them. I saw them just after I opened my mouth to try to breathe. Water rushed in, and everything went black. The next thing I knew, I was sitting on the creek bank in the grass. I was cold and scared, trembling all over. Then I heard someone say, 'Here she is. I found her.' Then I saw my dad—he came running to me. He picked me up and hugged me. Everything felt like a bad dream, and then it was all over. I was safe in my daddy's arms."

Christy looked up into the face of the angel. She was radiant, almost more beautiful than Christy had ever imagined.

"You are indeed my guardian angel," Christy said softly. "Do angels have names? Or what should I call you?"

The angel smiled. "Oh yes, Christy, we have names. I'm sorry I didn't introduce myself sooner. My name is Angelica, but you can call me Angie for short. The other angel who pulled you from the river is Kandie. Look over to the golden stairway—you'll see Amanda and Tiffanie there.

"If you were to go up the stairway, you'd see two trumpeters. Their names are Wayne and Robert. We call Robert 'Robbie' for short. Then, passing through the gates of heaven, you would find St. Peter. Christy, there are many more angels, but we are the ones assigned to look after you."

Christy smiled, a mixture of relief and awe washing over her. "I'm glad to meet all of you. Truly glad. But I'm so confused. After everything you've told me, what about the other lives? Why was I seeing all those different people and watching them die? I really don't understand. Can you explain?"

Angie nodded. "I wondered when you were going to ask about that," she said gently. "It's complicated, but I'll try to explain it in a way you can understand."

"Remember when I told you about souls and their duties on Earth?"

Christy nodded, remembering the lessons.

"Good," Angie continued. "Now, when a soul completes its duties on Earth, it goes to a place called the Spirit World. There it waits for God to hand down new instructions. If no instructions are given, the spirit remains, and the Spirit World becomes its final resting place for all eternity. The Spirit World isn't a bad place—it's the closest thing to heaven you'll ever find.

"But for some unknown reason, your spirit doesn't want to go. It has been avoiding us for centuries. It simply wants to stay on Earth. We don't know why, but that is impossible. A spirit that stays on Earth can interfere with God's master plan. You see, everything God creates has a purpose. Some of His plans go astray, and He has to correct them. When He made the soul, He had one plan—but it went awry. From that came good and evil. God corrected the plan: the good spirits go to the Spirit World under His care, and the evil spirits are cast out, sent back to Earth to wander hopelessly for all eternity."

Angie looked deeply into Christy's eyes, reading her thoughts. "No, Christy, your spirit is certainly not evil. It is just… contrary. It wants to stay on Earth, and as long as people continue to die tragic deaths, your spirit will remain bound here. We've been tracking your spirit for centuries. God gave us instructions and told us we were on our own.

"We finally think we understand how it keeps evading us. Just as we were about to close in on your spirit, it would jump back into a past life. When we got close in that life, it would immediately return to your present life. Then we would follow, and it would jump again into another past life. Each time we closed in, it felt us closing in and immediately slipped into another life. That's how your spirit has been eluding capture all these years."

Christy looked up at Angie, confusion written all over her face. "Angie, I'm really confused. Why then did I live all those past lives?"

Angie smiled gently. "Christy, you didn't actually live them—at least, not physically. You only experienced them in your mind."

Christy dropped her head, thinking for a moment. "How can that be?" she asked finally.

"It's possible because you and your spirit are linked through your mind," Angie explained. "It knows your every thought. When your spirit leaped into a past life, in your mind, you went with it. The more it traveled back, the easier it became for it to avoid us. By the time we discovered which life it had entered, it was too late. The person whose life your spirit slipped into had died a tragic death, and your spirit leapt back to your present life."

Christy was silent for a long while. Angie studied her face and eyes, noticing the struggle to believe what she was hearing.

"What's wrong, Christy? Are you having a hard time trying to understand?" Angie asked gently.

Christy looked at her and whispered, "Yes… and no."

"Explain," Angie encouraged.

Christy took a deep breath. "Okay, I'll try. With all the past lives I've been in, almost all of them were short-lived. But when I got to Lizzy's life, I kept going back. Her life was so much longer than the rest… why? I don't understand."

Angie nodded. "That was because of the doctors. They had to hypnotize you. When you were in hypnosis, your spirit became very confused. As soon as we got close, it panicked. Your spirit realized its time was running out. After Lizzy died—and she's in heaven now—there was nowhere for it to hide. Your soul couldn't avoid us any longer. It got desperate. It had to find a way to escape, and it decided to take complete control of your mind. At that time, if your mother and husband hadn't cared for you and ensured you ate, you would most surely have died."

"After weeks of care, you grew physically and mentally stronger. Once your strength returned, you were able to fight the spirit and break free from its overpowering trance. When you regained control, you returned to reality briefly. But your spirit realized time was running out. It grew angry, almost desperate, and decided that the next time it tried, it would be the last. It needed you to die to move on, and it planned to take full control of you."

"So, the next time," Angie continued softly, "it struck with such force that you could not resist. It took over completely. You had no choice but to obey. But we were there. Your spirit had no idea we were so close. We were simply waiting… waiting for it to make the wrong move. And finally, it did."

"When you drove your car to the bridge and plunged it into the river," Angie began softly, "we were simply waiting for the right moment to intervene. As the car hit the water, you opened your eyes. The river became a black abyss, endless and consuming. The car kept sinking, and the deeper it went, the more life drained from you. You were fading fast.

We were there, watching over you, but we couldn't act until the exact moment. When your spirit began to lift from your body, we captured it. Normally, we could not have done this, but in this case, God gave us the knowledge and authority to capture your spirit and replace it with another one. Without a spirit, you would cease to exist—and your time on earth was not yet finished. This, Christy, is one of the small miracles God can perform."

Christy smiled and studied Angie's eyes. They twinkled like stars in the night sky, and for a moment, all her fear melted away. "Am I going to die?" she asked, her voice trembling slightly.

Angie took her hand and smiled warmly. "No, child. You are not going to die. Not right now, anyway. I am only permitted to tell you this: you will live a long and happy life. You will become a grandmother—and even a great-grandmother—before you enter heaven. And yes, Christy, you will be one of the special souls welcomed into heaven when your time comes.

But for now, you will return to earth and live a normal life. Yes, normal—no more voices, no more past lives. Only your life, your time."

Christy hesitated. "I… I won't know how to live a normal life," she admitted softly.

Angie squeezed her hand reassuringly. "Everything will be fine. You'll live each day like everyone else. Now, are you ready to go back?"

Christy looked around. Everything there was pure, serene, and beautiful—the outskirts of heaven itself. She thought of staying, of the peace and wonder, but then her heart turned to her family, and what they had endured. They could live without her, yes, but she could not bear the thought of putting them through any more pain. She wanted to see them again, especially the children. She missed them deeply.

"I'm ready to go home," she whispered to Angie.

CHAPTER
Eleven

A New Beginning

Angie and Kandie took Christy gently by the arms. She felt herself lifted from the clouds, floating with them through the soft, misty expanse. As they descended below the clouds, Christy looked down and gasped. The city below glowed in the rays of light streaming from the heavens, illuminating everything in a warm, golden glow. She saw the world from a perspective she had never known. Everything was magnificent—and for the first time in what felt like forever, Christy knew that everything was going to be just fine.

Below, Gene and Jake stood at the edge of the bridge, worn and anxious. The Coast Guard had been struggling to hook up cables to pull Christy's car from the river, and hours had passed since it went over the edge. Gene had given up hope of ever seeing her alive. He sat slumped on the bridge, thinking God had forsaken him, wondering why Christy had seemed so desperate to end her life.

The police came over, offering coffee and soft words of comfort. Gene and Jake accepted the coffee but barely noticed it. Then a shout came from the Coast Guard boat.

"Look up there!"

All eyes turned skyward. Once again, the heavens opened, and rays of light streamed down—but this time, they focused on the edge of the bridge. Gene and Jake stood in the middle of the glow, frozen in awe. From the radiance emerged a bluish-green haze. Slowly, forms began to take shape—Angie and Kandie, returning Christy safely to the earth. The crowd fell silent, spellbound.

The angels floated down gracefully, setting Christy gently on the bridge and turning her toward Gene. Angie reached out and touched his hand for a moment before the angels began to drift back toward the heavens. Then, suddenly, Angie returned, hovering beside Christy.

"Good luck," she said softly, kissing Christy on the cheek. Her eyes twinkled like starlight. "I'm going to miss you." She floated upward, pausing just before disappearing entirely. She blew Christy one last kiss and vanished like a flash of light.

Though Angie would miss her, she was content. She had returned Christy to the life and family who loved her. She knew she would always be Christy's guardian angel.

Gene, still in shock, gathered Christy into his arms. He held her so tightly it hurt, but she didn't mind. She, too, was overjoyed to be back. Gene turned to Jake, his face a mixture of disbelief and wonder.

"How can this be?" he asked.

Jake shook his head slowly. "I don't know. All I know is that God works in mysterious ways… and this is truly a miracle."

Gene looked back at Christy. "Are you alright?"

"I'm fine now," she said, her voice calm but filled with awe. "I have seen the face of death many times, and now I've seen the face of a new life. I have seen heaven, spoken with angels, and been given a second chance. All I want now is to go home."

Her eyes filled with longing. "Can we please go home? Heaven will be there when I'm ready. All I want is to see the children and hold them. I'll never leave them again."

As they turned toward Gene's car, a police officer approached Christy. "I need to get to the bottom of all this," he said.

Christy, exhausted, looked up at him and replied gently, "I'm very tired. It's been a very long and difficult night. Can we talk tomorrow? I'll tell you everything you want to know. But right now, all I want is to go home to my family."

The officer tried to argue, but Christy simply turned and walked away. He had no choice—either wait or place her under arrest. Realizing the situation was beyond explanation, he muttered to himself, *This is the craziest thing I've ever seen… and if I told anyone who didn't see it, they'd never believe me. I guess we'll work on it tomorrow.*

The police finished wrapping things up at the bridge and returned to the station. From that day forward, every officer who had witnessed the miracle became a true believer.

Gene opened the car door for Christy. He kissed her gently and began to cry, holding her tightly.

"Honey," Christy said softly, "we'll be okay now. No more voices. No more other lives. It's all behind us. All the rest… they lie at the bottom of the river. They're gone. Now we can live a normal life… and be a real family."

She kissed him, and Gene looked into her glowing face. Her eyes sparkled like the stars. In that moment, he knew she was right. They had been given a second chance at life—and they would make it count. With that thought in mind, he drove her home to their family.

A year passed, and happiness filled their lives. Life had been very good to them. Christy had just given birth to a beautiful baby girl, who seemed almost angelic. They named her Angelica—Angie for short.

And with that, a new chapter of love, hope, and family began… a beautiful beginning that promised a lifetime of joy.

***** THE END*****